JOY to the WORLD

Joy to the World

A

Family Christmas
Treasury

Selected, Edited, and Introduced by ANN KEAY BENEDUCE

Illustrated by GENNADY SPIRIN

ATHENEUM BOOKS *for* YOUNG READERS
NEW YORK   LONDON   TORONTO   SYDNEY   SINGAPORE

Atheneum Books for Young Readers
An imprint of Simon & Schuster Children's Publishing Division
1230 Avenue of the Americas
New York, New York 10020

Book design by Michael Nelson
Cover and title page calligraphy by Jeanyee Wong
Music engraving by Robert Sherwin
The text of this book is set in Bernhard Modern.
The illustrations are rendered in watercolor and colored pencil.

Printed in the United States of America
2 4 6 8 10 9 7 5 3 1

Page 173 constitutes an extension of this copyright page.

Library of Congress Cataloging-in-Publication Data
Joy to the world ; a family Christmas treasury /
selected, edited, and introduced by Ann Keay Beneduce ;
illustrated by Gennady Spirin.
p. cm.
Summary: A collection of stories, poems, and plays about Christmas,
arranged in the categories of "The Star," "The Manger," "The Gift Givers,"
"The Tree," and "Christmas Everywhere."
ISBN 0-689-82113-1
1. Christmas—Literary collections. [1. Christmas—Literary collections.]
I. Beneduce, Ann. II. Spirin, Gennady, ill.
PZ5.C4638 2000
808.8'0334 21—dc21
99-40002

FIRST EDITION

For Wendy, Cynthia, and Joel, with love
A. K. B.

For my wife, Raisa
G. S.

CONTENTS

JOY *to the* WORLD

SYMBOLS AND TRADITIONS OF CHRISTMAS

Christmas is a time for tradition, sacred and secular. It is a time for the reunion of beloved friends, the gathering together of families; it is a time for telling again the wonderful story of the birth of the Holy Child; it is also the time for decking the house with holly and ivy and setting up crèches and Christmas trees; for the sound of hymns and carols on the frosty night air; for stockings hung by the fireside; and for the making of new memories to shine down the ensuing years like Christmas candles in the heart.

Though more than two thousand years have passed since the night when Jesus Christ was born, the message He brought has never lost its relevance. The symbols of Christmas—the star, the

manger, the tree, the gifts—are as meaningful today as they were when the first "Christ's mass" was celebrated. And the promise of the angels on that momentous occasion still expresses the deepest hope of people everywhere for peace on Earth and good-will to all.

From its humble beginning in a manger in a small Middle Eastern city, the Christian community has grown and spread to virtually every country and culture in the world. The stories and songs in this book and the descriptions of Christmas customs past and present cannot pretend to be complete or all-encompassing, but they all express the spirit of reverence, of love, of wonder—and the very special joy that Christmas brings.

the STAR

the STAR

The star that shimmers at the top of the decorated, candlelit fir tree is a reminder of the first and perhaps the most familiar of all the symbols of Christmas: the star that guided the wise men on their journey from the East, the star that aroused the sleeping shepherds, filling them with awe and wonderment, the star that shone steadily and brightly over the humble stable in Bethlehem to announce to the world the birth of the Holy Child.

What kind of a star was it? one wonders. Mentioned in all the biblical accounts of the events surrounding the birth of Jesus, it must surely have been something out of the ordinary, a star of unusual brilliance. Astronomers of today can look back and

quite accurately describe the paths of the known stars over the past centuries and millennia. A well-equipped planetarium can reproduce the sky as it was on the night of December 25 in the year 1, when Jesus is customarily assumed to have been born. But the experts report that there was no remarkably bright star in the sky on that date.

What, then, could it have been? A meteor? No, for meteors are not rare at all. Furthermore, they disappear rapidly. A meteor could not have shone steadily for several months, as did the star that led the wise men. Perhaps a comet? No, astronomers say there was no comet in the sky at that time. Could it have been a *nova*, a new star? Again, the scientists have determined that no nova appeared at that time. But they do have another idea to suggest. They think we may be celebrating Christ's birthday on the wrong date.

The explanation requires a little detective work, and a careful reading of the events leading up to Christ's birth as described in the Bible and by historians close to that period.

They all agree that Herod was the king of Judaea when Christ was born, and that Herod feared that the Child would become a dangerous rival. They mention a partial eclipse of the moon when Herod died. Modern astronomers tell us that such an

eclipse occurred on March 13 in the year we would now call 4 B.C., which is now considered the year of Herod's death. So Jesus must have been alive as early as 4 B.C., but no more than two years old, as we know that in order to be sure to be rid of his infant rival, Herod decreed that all children of two years or under must be put to death.

We also have evidence that, in 8 B.C., the Roman emperor Caesar Augustus ordered that everyone under his rule must go to his own native city to be taxed. The Roman Empire was vast at that time. For many, this decree meant a long journey; one that could take months or even years. For Joseph and his family, who had to travel by foot or by donkey, it could have taken two years to reach Bethlehem. So it seems that sometime between 8 B.C. and the date of Herod's death in 4 B.C., Jesus was born, most probably in the year 6 B.C.

Astronomers now agree that in the year we call 6 B.C. there was an extraordinary event in the sky. Three planets—Mars, Jupiter, and Saturn—moved so close together, they formed a small triangle in the sky near the constellation Pisces. They stayed in this formation for several months. Could this have been the "star" that guided the wise men to the stable in Bethlehem where the newborn Jesus lay? Or was there, after all, a kind of

miracle, a "star of wonder" shining in the sky on that night of nights?

The stars are universal sources of wonder and inspiration, and legends and beliefs about them (as well as scientific theories) can be found in many cultures from the ancient Greeks to the Navajos, from Africa to Alaska. The Christian star is usually shown with five points, the Jewish Star of David has six, and the Moslem star has eight.

In Poland and some other parts of Europe, as well as in Russia and Iran, the celebration of Christmas begins with the appearance of the first star on Christmas Eve. In Scandinavia, Germany, Switzerland, and Alaska, a Star Boy, carrying a star-tipped wand, leads three boys dressed as the three kings, followed by a colorful procession of costumed children, through the village streets on Twelfth Night, the eve of Epiphany. In parts of Mexico and Latin America, on the Night of the Three Kings, a big, star-shaped *piñata* is carried at the head of a happy parade of children. At the end, the children can break open the piñata and share the sweets and small toys contained inside it.

The stars have always been symbols of hope and idealism. "*Ad astra per aspera* (Through hard work to the stars)," said the

ancient Romans. We look to the stars for our guidance and thank our "lucky stars" when fortune smiles on us. Gold stars for good performance gleam on children's report cards. But, above all, the Christmas star has become a joyful beacon to believers all over the earth, telling us that the Holy Child is born.

Now when Jesus was born in Bethlehem of Judaea in the days of Herod the king, behold, there came wise men from the east to Jerusalem.

Saying, Where is he that is born King of the Jews? for we have seen his star in the east, and are come to worship him.

When Herod the king had heard these things, he was troubled, and all Jerusalem with him.

And when he had gathered all the chief priests and scribes of the people together, he demanded of them where Christ should be born.

And they said unto him, In Bethlehem of Judaea: for thus it is written by the prophet,

And thou Bethlehem, in the land of Judaea, art not the least among the princes of Judaea: for out of thee shall come a Governor, that shall rule my people Israel.

Then Herod, when he had privily called the wise men, inquired of them diligently what time the star appeared.

And he sent them to Bethlehem, and said, Go and search diligently for the young child; and when ye have found him, bring me word again, that I may come and worship him also.

When they had heard the king, they departed; and, lo, the star, which they saw in the east, went before them, till it came and stood over where the young child was.

When they saw the star, they rejoiced with exceeding great joy.

Matthew 2:1–10

We Three Kings of Orient Are

John H. Hopkins, Jr., 1857   John H. Hopkins, Jr.

We three kings of O - ri - ent are, Bear-ing gifts we trav - erse far Field and foun-tain, moor and moun-tain, Fol-low-ing yon - der Star. Oh, __ star of won-der, star of might, Star with roy - al beau-ty bright, West-ward lead-ing, still pro-ceed-ing, Guide us to the per - fect light.

2. Born a babe on Bethlehem's plain,
   Gold we bring to crown Him again;
   King forever, ceasing never,
   Over us all to reign.
   Refrain

3. Frankincense to offer have I;
   Incense owns a Deity nigh,
   Pray'r and praising all men raising,
   Worship God on high.
   Refrain

4. Myrrh is mine; its bitter perfume
   Breathes a life of gath'ring gloom;
   Sorrowing, sighing, bleeding, dying,
   Sealed in the stone-cold tomb.
   Refrain

5. Glorious now behold Him rise,
   King and God and Sacrifice;
   Heav'n sings "Hallelujah!"
   "Hallelujah!" earth replies.
   Refrain

A CHRISTMAS CAROL

by Gilbert K. Chesterton

The Christ-child lay on Mary's heart,
His hair was like a fire.
(O weary, weary is the world,
But here is the world's desire.)

The Christ-child stood at Mary's knee,
His hair was like a crown,
And all the flowers looked up at Him,
And all the stars looked down.

The Christ-child lay on Mary's lap,
His hair was like a light.
(O weary, weary were the world,
But here is all aright.)

The Christ-child lay on Mary's breast,
His hair was like a star,
(O stern and cunning are the kings,
But here the true hearts are.)

Shepherd's Song
at Christmas

by Langston Hughes

Look there at the star!
I, among the least,
Will arise and take
A journey to the East.
But what shall I bring
As a present for the King?
What shall I bring to the Manger?
    I will bring a song,
    A song that I will sing,
    In the Manger.

Watch out for my flocks,
Do not let them stray.
I am going on a journey
Far, far away.
But what shall I bring
As a present for the Child?
What shall I bring to the Manger?
    I will bring a lamb,
    Gentle, meek, and mild,
    A lamb for the Child
    In the Manger.

THE FIRST NOËL

TRADITIONAL

Minstrel's Song

by Ted Hughes

I've just had an astounding dream as I lay in the straw.

I dreamed a star fell on to the straw beside me

And lay blazing. Then when I looked up

I saw a bull come flying through a sky of fire

And on its shoulders a huge silver woman

Holding the moon. And afterwards there came

A donkey flying through that same burning heaven

And on its shoulders a colossal man

Holding the sun. Suddenly I awoke

And saw a bull and a donkey kneeling in the straw,

And the great moving shadows of a man and a woman—

I say they were a man and a woman but

I dare not say what I think they were. I did not dare to look.

I ran out here into the freezing world

Because I dared not look. Inside that shed.

A star is coming this way along the road.
If I were not standing upright, this would be a dream.
A star the shape of a sword of fire, point-downward,
Is floating along the road. And now it rises.
It is shaking fire on to the roofs and the gardens.
And now it rises above the animal shed
Where I slept till the dream woke me. And now
The star is standing over the animal shed.

CHRISTMAS

by Faith Baldwin

The snow is full of silver light
Spilled from the heavens' tilted cup
And, on this holy, tranquil night,
The eyes of men are lifted up
To see the promise written fair,
The hope of peace for all on earth,
And hear the singing bells declare
The marvel of the dear Christ's birth.
The way from year to year is long
And though the road be dark so far,
Bright is the manger, sweet the song,
The steeple rises to the Star.

the MANGER

the MANGER

At the spiritual heart of all our Christmas celebrations is, of course, the story of the birth of Jesus as told with moving simplicity in the Gospels of Matthew and Luke, and retold each Yuletide in homes and churches great and small all over the world. Many beautiful hymns and carols about the nativity have also come to be a traditional part of church services on Christmas day.

As a reminder of this momentous event, many families set up a miniature nativity scene at home. Often called "mangers," these may be small or large and can range from the simplest handmade figurines to impressive displays of exquisite artistry. In addition to Mary, Joseph, and the newborn baby Jesus in his

humble manger bed, these usually include the awestruck shepherds and some of their flock, as well as the ox and ass, and also the Magi, the three wise men or kings from the East. In many communities, larger nativity scenes, featuring full-sized figures, are set up outside of churches. This custom probably began during the early centuries of Christianity as a means of bringing the story of Christ's birth to people who could not read.

In 1224, Saint Francis of Assisi devised another way to bring the Christmas story to the people of Greccio, a small town in Italy. In a nearby cave he had a manger scene set up, using real people and animals. (The Holy Child, though, was a life-sized wax doll.) On Christmas Eve he invited the farmers and shepherds and other villagers to come and bring their families to see and hear what may have been the first Christmas pageant ever.

There were also, in Europe in medieval times and later, strolling groups of players who wandered from town to town, acting out scenes from the life of Christ or dramatic accounts of saints, martyrs, and miracles. Though not necessarily directly related to the nativity, these were often performed at Christmastime or at its ending, on Twelfth Night, the eve of Epiphany. Twelfth Night became a traditional time for feasting

and revelry, and plays were sometimes commissioned especially to be performed at this time.

Nowadays, in addition to a manger scene (called a *crèche* in France, a *presepe* in Italy, a *Krippe* in Germany, and a *nacimiento, pesabre,* or *portale* in Spanish-speaking countries), a play or pageant is often part of the celebration of the nativity. This may be a "Passion Play" based on a medieval source, like the *pastorelas* in Mexico and parts of the United States, or an opera, like Gian-Carlo Menotti's *Amahl and the Night Visitors,* or a performance of the ballet *The Nutcracker,* based on E. T. A. Hoffmann's story, but very often these days it is an enactment by children of the biblical account of Christ's birth.

AND IT CAME TO PASS IN THOSE DAYS, THAT THERE WENT out a decree from Caesar Augustus, that all the world should be taxed.

(And this taxing was first made when Cyrenius was governor of Syria.)

And all went to be taxed, every one into his own city.

And Joseph also went up from Galilee, out of the city of Nazareth, into Judaea, unto the city of David, which is called Bethlehem; (because he was of the house and lineage of David:)

To be taxed with Mary his espoused wife, being great with child.

And so it was, that, while they were there, the days were accomplished that she should be delivered.

And she brought forth her firstborn son, and wrapped him in swaddling clothes, and laid him in a manger; because there was no room for them in the inn.

Luke 2:1–7

THE BEST CHRISTMAS PAGEANT EVER

Excerpted from the book
THE BEST CHRISTMAS PAGEANT EVER

by Barbara Robinson

The six Herdman children, Ralph, Imogene, Gladys, LeRoy, Claude, and Ollie, who are notorious troublemakers at school, have nevertheless been chosen to play the leading roles in the Sunday school pageant by the narrator's mother, who is in charge of the program this year.

On the night of the pageant we didn't have any supper because Mother forgot to fix it. My father said that was all right. Between Mrs. Armstrong's telephone calls and the pageant rehearsals, he didn't expect supper anymore.

"When it's all over," he said, "we'll go someplace and have hamburgers." But Mother said when it was all over she might want to go someplace and hide.

"We've never once gone through the whole thing," she said. "I

don't know what's going to happen. It may be the first Christmas pageant in history where Joseph and the Wise Men get in a fight, and Mary runs away with the baby."

She might be right, I thought, and I wondered what all of us in the angel choir ought to do in case that happened. It would be dumb for us just to stand there singing about the Holy Infant if Mary had run off with him.

But nothing seemed very different at first.

There was the usual big mess all over the place—baby angels getting poked in the eye by other baby angels' wings and grumpy shepherds stumbling over their bathrobes. The spotlight swooped back and forth and up and down till it made you sick at your stomach to look at it and, as usual, whoever was playing the piano pitched "Away in a Manger" so high we could hardly hear it, let alone sing it. My father says "Away in a Manger" always starts out sounding like a closet full of mice.

But everything settled down, and at 7:30 the pageant began.

While we sang "Away in a Manger," the ushers lit candles all around the church, and the spotlight came on to be the star. So you really had to know the words to "Away in a Manger" because you couldn't see anything—not even Alice Wendleken's vase-line eyelids.

After that we sang two verses of "O, Little Town of Bethlehem," and then we were supposed to hum some more "O, Little Town of Bethlehem" while Mary and Joseph came in from a side door. Only they didn't come right away. So we hummed and hummed and hummed, which is boring and also very hard, and before long doesn't sound like any song at all—more like an old refrigerator.

"I knew something like this would happen," Alice Wendleken whispered to me. "They didn't come at all! We won't have any Mary and Joseph—and now what are we supposed to do?"

I guess we would have gone on humming till we all turned blue, but we didn't have to. Ralph and Imogene were there all right, only for once they didn't come through the door pushing each other out of the way. They just stood there for a minute as if they weren't sure they were in the right place—because of the candles, I guess, and the church being full of people. They looked like the people you see on the six o'clock news—refugees, sent to wait in some strange ugly place, with all their boxes and sacks around them.

It suddenly occurred to me that this was just the way it must have been for the real Holy Family, stuck away in a barn by people who didn't much care what happened to them. They couldn't have been very neat and tidy either, but more like *this*

Mary and Joseph (Imogene's veil was cockeyed as usual, and Ralph's hair stuck out all around his ears). Imogene had the baby doll but she wasn't carrying it the way she was supposed to, cradled in her arms. She had it slung up over her shoulder, and before she put it in the manger she thumped it twice on the back.

I heard Alice gasp and she poked me. "I don't think it's very nice to burp the baby Jesus," she whispered, "as if he had colic." Then she poked me again. "Do you suppose he *could* have had colic?"

I said, "I don't know why not," and I didn't. He could have had colic, or been fussy, or hungry like any other baby. After all, that was the whole point of Jesus—that he didn't come down on a cloud like something out of "Amazing Comics," but that he was born and lived . . . a real person.

Right away we had to sing "While Shepherds Watched Their Flocks by Night"—and we had to sing very loud, because there were more shepherds than there were anything else, and they made so much noise, banging their crooks around like a lot of hockey sticks.

Next came Gladys, from behind the angel choir, pushing people out of the way and stepping on everyone's feet. Since Gladys was the only one in the pageant who had anything to say she made the most of it: "Hey! Unto you a child is born!" she hollered, as if it was, for sure, the best news in the world. And all

the shepherds trembled, sore afraid—of Gladys, mainly, but it looked good anyway.

Then came three carols about angels. It took that long to get the angels in because they were all primary kids and they got nervous and cried and forgot where they were supposed to go and bent their wings in the door and things like that.

We got a little rest then, while the boys sang "We Three Kings of Orient Are," and everybody in the audience shifted around to watch the Wise Men march up the aisle.

"What have they got?" Alice whispered.

I didn't know, but whatever it was it was heavy—Leroy almost dropped it. He didn't have his frankincense jar either, and Claude and Ollie didn't have anything although they were supposed to bring the gold and the myrrh.

"I knew this would happen," Alice said for the second time. "I bet it's something awful."

"Like what?"

"Like . . . a burnt offering. You know the Herdmans."

Well, they did burn things, but they hadn't burned this yet. It was a ham—and right away I knew where it came from. My father was on the church charitable works committee—they give away food baskets at Christmas, and this was the Herdmans' food-basket ham. It still had the ribbon around it, saying Merry Christmas.

"I'll bet they stole that!" Alice said.

"They did not. It came from their food basket, and if they want to give away their own ham I guess they can do it." But even if the Herdmans didn't *like* ham (that was Alice's next idea) they had never before in their lives given anything away except lumps on the head. So you had to be impressed.

Leroy dropped the ham in front of the manger. It looked funny to see a ham there instead of the fancy bath-salts jars we always used for the myrrh and the frankincense. And then they went and sat down in the only space that was left.

While we sang "What Child Is This?" the Wise Men were supposed to confer among themselves and then leave by a different door, so everyone would understand that they were going home another way. But the Herdmans forgot, or didn't want to, or something, because they didn't confer and they didn't leave either. They just sat there, and there wasn't anything anyone could do about it.

"They're ruining the whole thing!" Alice whispered, but they weren't at all. As a matter of fact, it made perfect sense for the Wise Men to sit down and rest, and I said so.

"They're supposed to have come a long way. You wouldn't

expect them just to show up, hand over the ham, and leave!"

As for ruining the whole thing, it seemed to me that the Herdmans had improved the pageant a lot, just by doing what came naturally—like burping the baby, for instance, or thinking a ham would make a better present than a lot of perfumed oil.

Usually, by the time we got to "Silent Night," which was always the last carol, I was fed up with the whole thing and couldn't wait for it to be over. But I didn't feel that way this time. I almost wished for the pageant to go on, with the Herdmans in charge, to see what else they would do that was different.

Maybe the Wise Men would tell Mary about their problem with Herod, and she would tell them to go back and lie their heads off. Or Joseph might go with them and get rid of Herod once and for all. Or Joseph and Mary might ask the Wise Men to take the Christ Child with them, figuring that no one would think to look there.

I was so busy planning new ways to save the baby Jesus that I missed the beginning of "Silent Night," but it was all right because everyone sang "Silent Night," including the audience. We sang all the verses too, and when we got to "Son of God, Love's pure light" I happened to look at Imogene and I almost dropped my hymn book on a baby angel.

Everyone had been waiting all this time for the Herdmans to do something absolutely unexpected. And sure enough, that was what happened.

Imogene Herdman was crying.

In the candlelight her face was all shiny with tears and she didn't even bother to wipe them away. She just sat there—awful old Imogene— in her crookedy veil, crying and crying.

Well. It *was* the best Christmas pageant we ever had.

Everybody said so, but nobody seemed to know why. When it was over people stood around the lobby of the church talking about what was different this year. There was something special, everyone said—they couldn't put their finger on what.

Mrs. Wendleken said, "Well, Mary the mother of Jesus had a black eye; that was something special. But only what you might expect," she added.

She meant that it was the most natural thing in the world for a Herdman to have a black eye. But actually nobody hit Imogene and she didn't hit anyone else. Her eye wasn't really black either, just all puffy and swollen. She had walked into the corner of the choir-robe cabinet, in a kind of daze—as if she had just caught onto the idea of God, and the wonder of Christmas.

And this was the funny thing about it all. For years, I'd

thought about the wonder of Christmas, and the mystery of Jesus' birth, and never really understood it. But now, because of the Herdmans, it didn't seem so mysterious after all.

When Imogene had asked me what the pageant was about, I told her it was about Jesus, but that was just part of it. It was about a new baby, and his mother and father who were in a lot of trouble—no money, no place to go, no doctor, nobody they knew. And then, arriving from the East (like my uncle from New Jersey) some rich friends.

But Imogene, I guess, didn't see it that way. Christmas just came over her all at once, like a case of chills and fever. And so she was crying, and walking into the furniture.

Afterward there were candy canes and little tiny Testaments for everyone, and a poinsettia plant for my mother from the whole Sunday school. We put the costumes away and folded up the collapsible manger, and just before we left, my father snuffed out the last of the tall white candles.

"I guess that's everything," he said as we stood at the back of the church. "All over now. It was quite a pageant."

AWAY IN A MANGER

ATTRIBUTED TO MARTIN LUTHER

FIFTEENTH-CENTURY GERMAN

Dolce

1. A - way in a man - ger no crib for a bed, The
2. The cat - tle are low - ing, the poor ba - by wakes, But

lit - tle Lord Je - sus laid down His sweet head, The
lit - tle Lord Je - sus, no cry - ing He makes, I

stars in the sky, looked down where He lay, The
love Thee, Lord Je - sus, look down from the sky, And

lit - tle Lord Je - sus, a - sleep on the hay.
stay by my cra - dle, till morn - ing is nigh.

3. Be near me, Lord Jesus,
   I ask Thee to stay
   Close by me forever,
   And love me, I pray;
   Bless all the dear children
   In Thy tender care,
   And take us to heaven
   To live with Thee there.

A Little Child

Anonymous

A little child,
    A shining star,
A stable rude,
    The door ajar,

Yet in this place,
    So crude, forlorn,
The Hope of all
    The world was born.

The Mother's Song

Eskimo poem, translated by Peter Freuchen

It is so still in the house.
There is a calm in the house;
The snowstorm wails out there,
And the dogs are rolled up with snouts under tails.
My little boy is sleeping on the ledge,
On his back he lies, breathing through his open mouth.
His little stomach is bulging round—
Is it strange if I start to cry with joy?

36

WHAT CHILD IS THIS?

William C. Dix

Old English Air, "Greensleeves"

Moderato

mf

What Child is this, __ Who, laid to rest __ On Ma - ry's lap __ is

sleep-ing? Whom an-gels greet with an-thems sweet, While shep-herds watch are keep-ing?

ff

This, this __ is Christ the King; Whom shep-herds guard and an - gels sing:

Haste, haste __ to bring Him laud, __ The Babe, __ the Son __ of Ma - ry!

2. Why lies He in such mean estate,
   Where ox and ass are feeding?
   Good Christian, fear: for sinner here
   The silent Word is pleading:
   Refrain

3. So bring Him incense, gold and myrrh,
   Come peasant, king to own Him;
   The King of kings salvation brings;
   Let loving hearts enthrone Him.
   Refrain

THE COVENTRY CAROL

ROBERT CROO, 1534

ENGLISH MELODY, 1591

Slowly, tenderly

1. Lul - lay, Thou lit - tle ti - ny Child, Bye, bye, lul - ly, lul - lay; Lul - lay, Thou lit - tle ti - ny Child, Bye, bye, lul - ly, lul - lay.

2. O sis - ters, too, how may we do, For to pre - serve this day; This poor Young - ling for whom we sing, Bye, bye, lul - ly, lul - lay.

3. Herod the King, in his raging,
   Charged he hath this day;
   His men of might, in his own sight,
   All children young to slay.

4. Then woe is me, poor Child, for thee,
   And ever mourn and say;
   For thy parting nor say nor sing,
   Bye, bye, lully, lullay.

38

Silent Night

JOSEPH MÖHR, 1818

FRANZ GRÜBER, 1818

Si – lent night! Ho – ly night! All is calm, all is bright.

'Round yon vir – gin moth-er and child! Ho – ly In – fant, so ten – der and mild,

Sleep in heav – en-ly peace, ___ Sleep __ in heav – en-ly peace. ___

2. Silent night! Holy night!
   Shepherds quake at the sight!
   Glories stream from heaven afar,
   Heav'nly hosts sing "Alleluia!"
   Christ, the Savior, is born!
   Christ, the Savior, is born!

3. Silent night! Holy night!
   Son of God, love's pure light!
   Radiant beams from Thy holy face
   With the dawn of redeeming grace,
   Jesus, Lord at Thy birth,
   Jesus, Lord at Thy birth.

The Friendly Beasts

English, Traditional

Legend has it that on midnight of the night when Christ was born, all the animals were miraculously able to speak. It is also said that to this day, if no one is watching, all domestic animals kneel for a few moments at that hour. In England and parts of northern Europe there are stories of animals dancing for joy on Christmas Eve around a fir tree that glows with a magical light. In Spain, grandmothers tell how the gift of speech was first given to the animals in the stable—and then lost again when one vain little donkey took the occasion to brag about himself so loudly that he woke the sleeping baby. But in this beloved carol from twelfth-century England, the spell is not yet broken, and the kindly animals tell of their loving service to the newborn Jesus.

Jesus our brother, strong and good,
Was humbly born in a stable rude,
And the friendly beasts around Him stood,
Jesus our brother, strong and good.

"I," said the donkey, shaggy and brown,
"I carried His mother uphill and down,
I carried her safely to Bethlehem town;
I," said the donkey shaggy and brown.

"I," said the cow, all white and red,
"I gave Him my manger for His bed,
I gave Him my hay to pillow His head,
I," said the cow all white and red.

"I," said the sheep with curly horn,
"I gave Him my wool for His blanket warm,
He wore my coat on Christmas morn;
I," said the sheep with curly horn.

"I," said the dove, from the rafters high,
"Cooed Him to sleep, my mate and I;
We cooed Him to sleep, my mate and I;
I," said the dove, from the rafters high.

And every beast by some good spell,
In the stable dark was glad to tell,
Of the gift he gave Immanuel,
The gift he gave Immanuel.

O Little Town of Bethlehem

PHILLIPS BROOKS, 1868

LEWIS H. REDNER, 1868

1. O lit-tle town of Beth-le-hem, How still we see thee lie;
2. For Christ is born of Ma-ry; And gath-ered all a-bove,

A-bove thy deep and dream-less sleep The si-lent stars go by:
While mor-tals sleep, the an-gels keep Their watch of wond'ring love.

Yet in thy dark streets shin-eth The ev-er-last-ing Light;
O morn-ing stars to-geth-er Pro-claim the ho-ly birth;

The hopes and fears of all the years Are met in thee to-night.
And prais-es sing to God, the King, And peace to men on earth.

3. How silently, how silently,
   The wondrous gift is giv'n!
   So God imparts to human hearts
   The blessings of His heav'n.
   No ear may hear His coming,
   But in this world of sin,
   Where meek souls will receive Him, still
   The dear Christ enters in.

4. O holy child of Bethlehem,
   Descend to us, we pray;
   Cast out our sin, and enter in,
   Be born in us today.
   We hear the Christmas angels
   The great glad tidings tell;
   O come to us, abide with us,
   Our Lord Emmanuel.

A CHRISTMAS CAROL

English, Traditional

Before the paling of the stars,
    Before the winter morn,
Before the earliest cock-crow
    Jesus Christ was born:
    Born in a stable,
    Cradled in a manger,
In the world His hands had made
    Born a stranger.

Priest and king lay fast asleep
    In Jerusalem,
Young and old lay fast asleep
    In crowded Bethlehem:
Saint and angel, ox and ass,
    Kept a watch together,
Before the Christmas daybreak
    In the winter weather.

the **GIFT GIVERS**

the GIFT GIVERS

In the United States and in many other countries around the world, the idea of Christmas is almost inevitably accompanied by thoughts of Santa Claus, the beloved bringer of gifts to children. Of course, it was the Magi, the wise men, who were the first Christmas givers—the three kings from the East who brought precious offerings of frankincense, gold, and myrrh to honor the newborn king, the baby Jesus. But the present-day custom of giving gifts at Christmas seems more closely associated with the secular traditions that surround this joyous holiday than with its religious origin.

Though Santa Claus, the jolly old man in a red suit with a pack of toys on his back, is a fairly recent arrival on the

Christmas scene, his cultural ancestry can be traced back to the fourth century A.D., to a holy man known as Saint Nicholas, the bishop of Myra.

Nicholas was born in about 280 A.D., in the little town of Patara, in what is now a part of Turkey. He was a studious, religious boy, the beloved only child of fairly well-to-do Christian parents. When he was about twelve, unfortunately, his parents died of the plague, leaving him an orphan. However, Nicholas steadfastly continued his religious studies and after a few years was ordained a priest in the Christian church. At the early age of nineteen he was made Bishop of Myra, a nearby city. Nicknamed "the Boy Bishop," Nicholas was well-loved and known to be wise and kind, and he attracted many converts to the Christian faith. But in the year 303, the Roman emperor Diocletian declared himself to be a god and ordered all citizens to worship him as such. Many Christians, including Nicholas, resisted this, as it was against their belief to worship any other god than their own. For their disobedience, thousands of Christians were punished and imprisoned by their Roman rulers. Nicholas was confined to a small cell and suffered a great deal. Finally, in 313, a new emperor, Constantine the Great, came into power. He released

all the Christians who had been imprisoned for their beliefs, including Nicholas, who went back to his church in Myra and continued his work as a bishop. When he died, he was buried in Myra. In 1087, his remains were taken to Bari, Italy, where they are still enshrined in the eleventh-century basilica of S. Nicola.

Legends of this generous, kindly saint abound, and many miracles are attributed to him. One tells of three boys who were murdered by an innkeeper, who cut their bodies into pieces and hid their remains in a pickle barrel. But at Nicholas's command, the three lads stepped out of the barrel in perfect health. Word of this and other miracles spread and multiplied, even after his death, and over the centuries Nicholas was adopted as the patron saint of children, of sailors, of young women hoping to marry, and of countries such as Russia and Greece. Thousands of churches are dedicated to him, and his name day, December 6, is celebrated widely. His miracles and good deeds were the subjects of many medieval plays and pageants in Europe, especially in France, where the story of the three boys' murder and resurrection was—and still is—a particular favorite.

Another of Nicholas's good deeds is an even more popular

subject of dramas performed on his name day, December 6, or during the Christmas season in Europe. It is said that in a village near Myra there lived a man, a widower, with three lovely daughters. The father hoped for his daughters to marry well, but he had fared poorly in business and had lost all his money, so he could not provide his daughters with dowries. Saint Nicholas heard about his plight and wanted to give him some money, but he knew the man would be too proud to accept charity from him. So the good saint came to their house at night and threw bags full of gold coins in through the open window. In one version of the story, the daughters had washed their stockings and hung them by the fireplace to dry. The bags of money thrown in by Nicholas landed right in these stockings, where they were found the next morning by the surprised maidens. Needless to say, the young women were overjoyed, and all of them married well. When people heard about this, they began honoring the generous saint by imitation, giving presents to others in need. Gradually Saint Nicholas, with his reputation as a gift giver, became the patron saint of Christmas. And gift giving moved beyond charity to become a happy custom among families and friends at Christmastime. Probably our Christmas Eve tradition of

hanging stockings in front of the fireplace to be filled by Saint Nicholas also comes from this old legend.

Over the centuries, Saint Nicholas became known in Holland as Sinter Claes, a benevolent character who brought toys to "good" children. In the seventeenth century this tradition came with the first Dutch settlers to New Amsterdam (as they called what is now New York). His name gradually evolved to Santa Claus in the United States and some other countries, and his personality became that of the familiar gift giver we know today.

But Santa Claus did not take on his modern stature until about the middle of the nineteenth century. Before that time, he was quite small, and one could easily imagine him sliding down the chimney. As late as 1824, when Dr. Clement Moore's poem "A Visit from Saint Nicholas" was published, it described him as a "jolly old elf" flying through the air in "a miniature sleigh" drawn by "eight tiny reindeer." It was not until 1863, when the American artist Thomas Nast drew him as a full-sized man in a red suit trimmed with white fur and a red hat to match, that he finally took on the appearance we are familiar with today.

And when they were come into the house, they saw the young child with Mary his mother, and fell down and worshipped him: and when they had opened their treasures, they presented unto him gifts; gold, and frankincense, and myrrh.

Matthew 2:11

What Can I Give Him?

by Christina Rossetti

What can I give Him
    Poor as I am?
If I were a shepherd
    I would bring a lamb,
If I were a wise man
    I would do my part—
Yet what can I give Him?
    Give my heart.

CAROL OF THE BROWN KING

by Langston Hughes

Of the three Wise Men
Who came to the King,
One was a brown man,
So they sing.

Of the three Wise Men
Who followed the Star,
One was a brown king
From afar.

They brought fine gifts
Of spices and gold
In jeweled boxes
Of beauty untold.

Unto His humble
Manger they came
And bowed their heads
In Jesus' name.

Three Wise Men,
One dark like me—
Part of His
Nativity.

THE GIFT OF THE MAGI

by O. Henry

One dollar and eighty-seven cents. That was all. Della stood by the window and looked out dully at a gray cat walking a gray fence in a gray back yard. Tomorrow would be Christmas Day, and she had only $1.87 with which to buy Jim a present. She had been saving every penny she could for months, with this result. Twenty dollars a week doesn't go far. Expenses had been greater than she had calculated. They always are. Only $1.87 to buy a present for Jim. Her Jim. Many a happy hour she had spent planning for something nice for him. Something fine and rare and sterling—something just a little bit near to being worthy of the honor of being owned by Jim.

There was a pier glass between the windows of her room. Della suddenly whirled from the window and stood before the glass. Her eyes were shining brilliantly, but her face had lost its color within twenty seconds. Rapidly she pulled down her hair and let it fall to its full length. Now there were two possessions of the James Dillingham Youngs in which they both took a mighty pride. One was Jim's gold watch that had been his father's and his grandfather's. The other was Della's hair. Had the Queen of Sheba lived in the flat across the airshaft, Della would have let her hair hang out the window some day to dry just to depreciate Her Majesty's jewels and gifts. Had King Solomon been the janitor, with all his treasures piled up in the basement, Jim would have pulled out his watch every time he passed, just to see him pluck at his beard from envy.

So now Della's beautiful hair fell about her, rippling and shining like a cascade of brown waters. She did it up again nervously and quickly. Once she faltered for a minute while a tear splashed on the worn red carpet.

On went her old brown jacket; on went her old brown hat. With a whirl of skirts and with the brilliant sparkle still in her eyes, she fluttered out the door and down the stairs to the street.

Where she stopped the sign read: "Mme. Sofronie. Hair Goods of All Kinds." One flight up Della ran, and collected herself, panting. Madame, large, too white, chilly, hardly looked the "Sofronie."

"Will you buy my hair?" asked Della.

"I buy hair," said Madame. "Take yer hat off and let's have a sight at the looks of it."

Down rippled the brown cascade.

"Twenty dollars," said Madame, lifting the mass with a practiced hand.

"Give it to me quick," said Della.

Oh, and the next two hours tripped on rosy wings. Forget the hashed metaphor. She was ransacking the stores for Jim's present.

She found it at last. It surely had been made for Jim and no one else. There was no other like it in any of the stores, and she had turned all of them inside out. It was a platinum watch-chain, simple and chaste in design, properly proclaiming its value by substance alone and not by meretricious ornamentation—as all good things should do. It was even worthy of The Watch. As soon as she saw it she knew that it must be Jim's. It

JOY *to the* WORLD

was like him. Quietness and value—the description applied to both. Twenty-one dollars they took from her for it, and she hurried home with the eighty-seven cents. With that chain on his watch Jim might be properly anxious about the time in any company. Grand as the watch was, he sometimes looked at it on the sly on account of the shabby old leather strap that he used in place of a proper gold chain.

When Della reached home her intoxication gave way a little to prudence and reason. She got out her curling-irons and lighted the gas and went to work repairing the ravages made by generosity added to love.

Within forty minutes her head was covered with tiny close-lying curls that made her look wonderfully like a truant school-boy. She looked at her reflection in the mirror long, carefully, and critically.

"If Jim doesn't kill me," she said to herself, "before he takes a second look at me, he'll say I look like a Coney Island chorus girl. But what could I do—oh! what could I do with a dollar and eighty-seven cents?"

At seven o'clock the coffee was made and the frying-pan was on the back of the stove, hot and ready to cook the chops.

Jim was never late. Della doubled the watch chain in her hand and sat on the corner of the table near the door that he always entered. Then she heard his step on the stair away down on the first flight, and she turned white for just a moment. She had a habit of saying little silent prayers about the simplest everyday things, and now she whispered: "Please, God, make him think I am still pretty."

Jim stepped inside the door, as immovable as a setter at the scent of quail. His eyes were fixed upon Della, and there was an expression in them that she could not read, and it terrified her. It was not anger, nor surprise, nor disapproval, nor horror, nor any of the sentiments that she had been prepared for. He simply stared at her fixedly with that peculiar expression on his face.

"Jim, darling," cried Della, "don't look at me that way. I had my hair cut off and sold it because I couldn't have lived through Christmas without giving you a present. It'll grow out again— you won't mind, will you? I just had to do it. My hair grows awfully fast. Say 'Merry Christmas!' Jim, and let's be happy. You don't know what a nice—what a beautiful, nice gift I've got for you."

"You've cut off your hair?" asked Jim, laboriously, as if he had

not arrived at that patent fact yet even after the hardest mental labor.

"Cut it off and sold it," said Della. "Don't you like me just as well, anyhow?"

Jim looked about the room curiously.

"You say your hair is gone?" he said, with an air almost of idiocy.

"You needn't look for it," said Della. "It's sold, I tell you—sold and gone, too. It's Christmas Eve, boy. Be good to me, for it went for you. Maybe the hairs of my head were numbered," she went on with a sudden serious sweetness, "but nobody could ever count my love for you. Shall I put the chops on, Jim?"

Jim drew a package from his overcoat pocket and threw it upon the table.

"Don't make any mistake, Dell," he said, "about me. I don't think there's anything in the way of a haircut or a shave or a shampoo that could make me like my girl any less. But if you'll unwrap the package you may see why you had me going awhile at first."

White fingers and nimble tore at the string and paper. And then an ecstatic scream of joy; and then, alas! a quick feminine

change to hysterical tears and wails, necessitating the immediate employment of all the comforting powers of the lord of the flat.

For there lay The Combs—the set of combs that Della had worshiped for long in a Broadway window. Beautiful combs, pure tortoise shell, with jeweled rims—just the shade to wear in the beautiful vanished hair. They were expensive combs, she knew, and her heart had simply craved and yearned over them without the least hope of possession. And now they were hers, but the tresses that should have adorned the coveted adornments were gone.

But she hugged them to her bosom, and at length she was able to look up with dim eyes and a smile and say: "My hair grows so fast, Jim!"

And then Della leaped up like a little singed cat and cried, "Oh, oh!"

Jim had not yet seen his beautiful present. She held it out to him eagerly upon her open palm. This dull precious metal seemed to flash with a reflection of her bright and ardent spirit.

"Isn't it a dandy, Jim? I hunted all over town to find it. You'll have to look at the time a hundred times a day now. Give me your watch. I want to see how it looks on it."

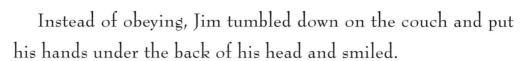

Instead of obeying, Jim tumbled down on the couch and put his hands under the back of his head and smiled.

"Dell," said he, "let's put our Christmas presents away and keep 'em awhile. They're too nice to use just at present. I sold the watch to get the money to buy your combs. And now suppose you put the chops on."

The Magi, as you know, were wise men—wonderfully wise men—who brought gifts to the Babe in the manger. They invented the art of giving Christmas presents. Being wise, their gifts were no doubt wise ones, possibly bearing the privilege of exchange in case of duplication. And here I have lamely related to you the uneventful chronicle of two foolish children in a flat who most unwisely sacrificed for each other the greatest treasures of their house. But in a last word to the wise of these days let it be said that of all who give gifts these two were the wisest. Of all who give and receive gifts, such as they are the wisest. Everywhere they are the wisest. They are the Magi.

{Note: This story has been slightly abridged, but is told entirely in the author's own words.}

Yes, Virginia

by Francis Church

On September 21, 1897, Francis Church, an editorial writer for the newspaper the New York Sun, *received this letter:*

Dear Editor:

I am eight years old. Some of my little friends say there is no Santa Claus. Papa says "If you see it in the *Sun* it's so." Please tell me the truth, is there a Santa Claus?

> Virginia O'Hanlon,
> 215 West 95th Street
> New York City

Here is Francis Church's reply:

Virginia, your little friends are *wrong.* They have been affected by the skepticism of a skeptical age. They do not *believe* except they *see.* They think that nothing can be which is not comprehensible by their little minds. All minds, Virginia, whether they be men's or children's are

little. In this great universe of ours man is a mere insect, an ant, in his intellect, as compared with the boundless world about him, as measured by the intelligence capable of grasping the whole of truth and knowledge.

Yes, Virginia, there *is* a Santa Claus. He exists as certainly as love, and generosity and devotion exist, and you know that they abound and give to your life its highest beauty and joy. Alas! How dreary would be the world if there were no Santa Claus! It would be as dreary as if there were no Virginias. There would be no childlike faith, then, no

poetry, no romance to make tolerable this existence. We should have no enjoyment, except in sense and sight. The Eternal light with which childhood fills the world would be extinguished.

Not believe in *Santa Claus*! You might as well not believe in fairies! You might get your papa to hire men to watch in all the chimneys on Christmas Eve to catch Santa Claus, but even if they did not see Santa Claus coming down what would that prove? Nobody sees Santa Claus, but that is no sign that there is no Santa Claus. The most real things in the world are those

that neither children nor men can see. Did you ever see fairies dancing on the lawn? Of course not, but that's no proof that they are not there. Nobody can conceive or imagine all the wonders there are unseen and unseeable in the world.

You tear apart the baby's rattle and see what makes the noise inside, but there is a veil covering the unseen world which not the strongest man, nor even the united strength of all the strongest men that ever lived, could tear apart. Only faith, fancy, poetry, love, romance, can push aside that curtain and view—and picture the supernal beauty and glory beyond. Is it all real? Ah, Virginia, in all this world there is nothing else real and abiding.

No Santa Claus! Thank God he lives, and he lives forever. A thousand years from now, Virginia, nay, ten times ten thousand years from now, he will continue to make glad the heart of childhood.

THE NIGHT BEFORE CHRISTMAS

by Clement C. Moore

Dr. Clement C. Moore, who wrote this poem, was born in New York City in 1779. He was a well-known classical scholar, professor of Hebrew and Greek literature in the Protestant Episcopal Seminary in New York. He wrote "A Visit from Saint Nicholas" (as it was originally titled) for his own children, and was surprised and dismayed when it was published in a newspaper. Apparently a friend of his family had found it so charming that she sent it in to the journal, knowing that many other families would also enjoy it. At first, Dr. Moore felt it was beneath his dignity as a professor to admit that he was the author. It was many years before he did so. Now it is the only one of all his works for which he is known.

'Twas the night before Christmas, when all through the house
Not a creature was stirring, not even a mouse;
The stockings were hung by the chimney with care,
In hopes that Saint Nicholas soon would be there;

The children were nestled all snug in their beds,
While visions of sugar-plums danced in their heads;
And Mama in her 'kerchief, and I in my cap,
Had just settled our brains for a long winter's nap;

When out on the lawn there arose such a clatter,
I sprang from the bed to see what was the matter.
Away to the window I flew like a flash,
Tore open the shutters and threw up the sash.

The moon on the breast of the new-fallen snow
Gave the luster of mid-day to objects below,
When what to my wondering sight should appear
But a miniature sleigh, and eight tiny reindeer,

With a little old driver, so lively and quick,
I knew in a moment it must be St. Nick.
More rapid than eagles his coursers they came,
And he whistled, and shouted, and called them by name:

"Now *Dasher!* now, *Dancer!* now, *Prancer* and *Vixen!*
On, *Comet!* On, *Cupid!* on, *Donner* and *Blitzen!*
To the top of the porch! to the top of the wall!
Now dash away! dash away! dash away all!"

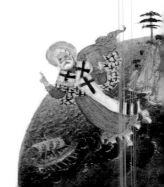

As dry leaves that before the wild hurricane fly,
When they meet with an obstacle, mount to the sky,
So up to the house-top the coursers they flew,
With the sleigh full of toys, and St. Nicholas too.

And then, in a twinkling, I heard on the roof
The prancing and pawing of each little hoof—
As I drew in my head and was turning around,
Down the chimney St. Nicholas came with a bound.

He was dressed all in fur from his head to his foot,
And his clothes were all tarnished with ashes and soot;
A bundle of toys he had flung on his back,
And he looked like a peddler just opening his pack.

His eyes—how they sparkled! his dimples how merry!
His cheeks were like roses, his nose like a cherry!
His droll little mouth was drawn up like a bow,
And the beard of his chin was as white as the snow;

The stump of a pipe he held tight in his teeth,
And the smoke it encircled his head like a wreath;
He had a broad face and a little round belly,
That shook when he laughed like a bowlful of jelly.

He was chubby and plump, a right jolly old elf,
And I laughed when I saw him, in spite of myself;
A wink of his eye and a twist of his head
Soon gave me to know I had nothing to dread.

He spoke not a word but went straight to his work,
And filled all the stockings; then turned with a jerk,
And laying his finger aside of his nose,
And giving a nod, up the chimney he rose;

He sprang to his sleigh, to his team gave a whistle,
And away they all flew like the down of a thistle.
But I heard him exclaim, ere he drove out of sight,

"Happy Christmas to all,
And to all a good night!"

THE BALLAD OF BEFANA

AN EPIPHANY LEGEND FROM ITALY

by Phyllis McGinley

Italian children know that the kindly old witch Befana will come while they are sleeping on the eve of Epiphany and leave them sweets and small toys. They have heard the story about that long-ago night when the three kings passed Befana's doorway and invited her to come with them to Bethlehem to worship the newborn baby Jesus. But the old woman refused, saying she was too busy cleaning her house. Later, when she changed her mind and tried to follow them, she lost her way and so she never saw the Holy Child. Every Epiphany eve since then the poor old woman has visited homes, leaving her small gifts and peering hopefully at the sleeping children, but she has never found the Child she is seeking.

Befana the Housewife, scrubbing her pane,
Saw three old sages ride down the lane,
Saw three gray travelers pass her door—
Gaspar, Balthazar, Melchior.

"Where journey you, sirs?" she asked of them.
Balthazar answered, "To Bethlehem,
For we have news of a marvelous thing.
Born in a stable is Christ the King."

"Give Him my welcome!"
Then Gaspar smiled,
"Come with us, mistress, to greet the Child."

"Oh, happily, happily would I fare,
Were my dusting through and I'd polished the stair."

Old Melchior leaned on his saddle horn,
"Then send but a gift to the small Newborn."

"Oh, gladly, gladly, I'd send Him one,
Were the hearthstone swept and my weaving done.

"As soon as ever I've baked my bread,
I'll fetch Him a pillow for His head,
And a coverlet, too," Befana said.

"When the rooms are aired and the linen dry,
I'll look at the Babe."
But the Three rode by.

She worked for a day and a night and a day,
Then gifts in her hands, took up her way.
But she never could find where the Christ Child lay.

And still she wanders at Christmastide,
Houseless, whose house was all her pride.

Whose heart was tardy, whose gifts were late;
Wanders, and knocks at every gate,
Crying, "Good people, the bells begin!
Put off your toiling and let love in."

THE BEST GIFT OF ALL

A PLAY FOR CHRISTMAS

by Mary Smith

Characters

 MARY

 NAOMI

 RUTH

 THE ANGEL

 MARTHA

OTHER CHILDREN

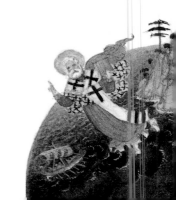

TIME: *The first Christmas Day.*

SETTING: *One of the roads that leads to Bethlehem.*

AT RISE: *A group of children are seen entering from the left.*

   Note: *These children may be all boys, or all girls, or boys and girls together. They may be of any and all ages. If all boys are used, the names may be changed. The children carry gifts for the Christ Child.*

———

RUTH: Aye. This is the road and we must hurry with our gifts.

MARTHA: Last night He was born in a manger in a stable. And today all the people are happy and we come bearing gifts for Him.

MARY: What are you bringing, Ruth? I'm bringing this fine vase. It is made of silver.

RUTH: I'm bringing an armband of gold. Rachel is bringing a jar of new sweet honey.

MARY: And my sister Elisabeth is bringing a fine toy; a lamb carved from wood. What are you bringing, Martha? (*Martha is the smallest girl in the crowd. At the question, she hangs her head.*)

RUTH: Yes, Martha, tell us.

MARTHA: I am bringing an apple. (*The other children look at each other.*) I polished it and polished it and now see—(*She takes*

79

an apple from the fold of her dress.) How it glows! Like a jewel.

RUTH: You mean—you mean—your gift is an *apple*?

MARTHA: Yes, I helped my mother all day and sang to the baby when he cried and brought my father his sandals when he came in from working in the fields. My mother rewarded me with this apple. It is the prettiest thing I have ever owned, and I am going to give it to the Christ Child.

MARY: Only an apple! Ha! Ha! Ha!

RUTH: That is no gift. Anyone can get an apple. You must bring silver or gold or sweet-smelling perfume. But an apple—Ha! Ha! Ha!

OTHER CHILDREN: She thinks it's a fine gift. (*All laugh.* Martha *looks unhappy.*)

MARTHA: I thought it looked so pretty. I did not eat it myself— although I wanted to. I wanted to save it as a gift.

RUTH: You are a very foolish girl. But come. We must hurry. (*All the children hurry off the right side.* Martha *stands still looking at the apple.*)

MARY: (*Running back*) But hurry, Martha, even if your gift is not so fine, we will tell how you did not keep it for yourself but saved it for a gift. Then your gift may be accepted, too.

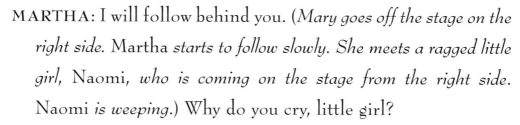

MARTHA: I will follow behind you. (*Mary goes off the stage on the right side. Martha starts to follow slowly. She meets a ragged little girl,* Naomi, *who is coming on the stage from the right side.* Naomi *is weeping*.) Why do you cry, little girl?

NAOMI: Because my mother is so poor, and I am so hungry. I have not had anything to eat all day. My little brother is lying in the fields. He, too, is crying because he is hungry. (*She cries again.*)

MARTHA: You must not cry. Today is a day of rejoicing. I am going into the city. There will be a great celebration. Perhaps you will find something to eat there. Come with me.

NAOMI: My brother is too little to walk so far. (*Sees the apple in* Martha's *hand.*) Oh how beautiful that is! Like a large ruby. How red and how round. And how good it must taste.

MARTHA: I am taking it to the Christ Child as a gift.

NAOMI: It will be the best of all the gifts.

MARTHA: My mother said that God made it. His sun warmed it into color. And the rain He sent made it sweet to taste. He made this out of a pretty sweet-smelling flower. Smell.

(Naomi *smells the apple.*)

NAOMI: It smells like the wind on a sunny day. How good it

must be to eat. But you must hurry. You must bring your fine gift to the city.

MARTHA: The other children laughed at me.

NAOMI: It will be the most beautiful gift of all.

MARTHA: I wish you would come with me.

NAOMI: I cannot. I am so hungry, and my brother is so small.

MARTHA (*Starts to follow after the other children.* Naomi *sits by the road and starts to cry. Just as* Martha *is about to go off the stage, she turn around and sees* Naomi *crying.* Martha *hurries back.*): Here, little girl. Take this apple. You are hungry. I cannot see you weep.

NAOMI: (*Joyfully*) But the gift—

MARTHA: I will listen to the stories that the other children tell of their gifts—

NAOMI: But this would be the finest gift of all.

MARTHA: There will be many gifts laid in the manger. But you are hungry. You must have this.

NAOMI: (*Taking it*) Oh thank you! Thank you! I will give my brother half and he will stop crying and be happy again. (Naomi *skips off happily with the apple.* Martha *sinks down on the side of the road and starts to cry. A beautiful* Angel *in a white robe appears.*)

ANGEL: Why do you weep, my child?

MARTHA: I gave my gift to a hungry child. And now I have no gift for the Christ Child. (*She cries harder. The* Angel *places her hand on* Martha's *head.*)

ANGEL: Do not weep. God has seen your gift to the hungry child. Because you thought of another and not of yourself, your gift is twice as precious as all the gold and silver, and sweet-smelling perfume. When you gave it to the hungry child it was as though you had given something precious to the Child Christ. So be comforted. Your gift was the best of all. (Martha *looks up with a smile, as the curtain falls.*)

CURTAIN

CHRISTMAS IS COMING

by Mother Goose (Anonymous)

Christmas is coming, the geese are
    getting fat,
Please to put a penny in an old
    man's hat;
If you haven't got a penny, a
    ha'penny will do,
If you haven't got a ha'penny,
    God bless you.

the _the_ TREE

the $\mathscr{T}$REE

The tree, whether a dazzling giant fir in a great city plaza or a small, simply decorated tree in a modest living room, is so much a part of our Christmas tradition that it is hard to realize that this has not always been so. Martin Luther is said to have originated the idea of the Christmas tree in Germany in the sixteenth century. One Christmas Eve, so the story goes, he was walking in the woods and was deeply impressed by the beauty of the pine trees against the star-filled sky. He cut a small pine tree and took it home to his family; he decorated its branches with lighted candles, which he said symbolized the starry sky over Bethlehem when Christ was born. His example was quickly imitated in Germany and throughout northern Europe. In Great Britain, however, this custom failed

to take root; the church at that time frowned on the traditional revels that had marked the year's end since ancient times. Most secular Christmas festivities were legally banned. And in Britain's American colonies, too, all popular celebration of Christmas was strictly forbidden by the early Puritan settlers. While these restrictions and bans were later lifted, their shadows lingered on. So the decorated Christmas tree as we know it now did not come into widespread acceptance in England and the United States until the mid-nineteenth century. Then Queen Victoria's German-born husband, Albert, on the birth of their son Edward VII in 1841, charmed the English court by having an evergreen tree brought into their home at Windsor Castle and decorated with colored glass ornaments and lighted candles. Gifts, beautifully wrapped, were placed under the tree, to be opened on Christmas Eve, as was already the custom in his native country. Once established in England, this festive custom soon spread to the United States and Canada, and eventually to most parts of the world. Now, Christmas without a tree is almost unthinkable.

Of course, evergreens and other trees have been a part of celebrations of the winter solstice since much earlier times, long before the birth of Christ. The Druids in ancient England and France decorated their sacred oaks with golden apples and lighted candles

at this time of year. The Romans, too, at their Saturnalia festivals in December, hung decorations and lighted candles on trees. Palm branches, symbolizing eternal life, were part of ancient Egyptian ceremonies for the end of winter. Some scholars associate the Christmas tree with Yggdrasil, the legendary Scandinavian "Tree of the Universe," which had one root in heaven and one root in hell. The old Norse name for the turning of the season, *Hweolar-tid*, evolved into the word *Yuletide*, which, as the northern tribes became Christians, came to be a term for *Christmastime.*

The candles or their electrical counterparts that shine on Christmas trees everywhere probably also have their origins in earlier times than Luther's. From time immemorial, winter solstice festivals everywhere have celebrated the return of the sun's light with candles and other lights. So it seems natural to think of this as one of the sources of our present-day custom. Another theory stems from the fact that on the night of Christ's birth, the windows of the houses of Bethlehem would surely have been glowing with Hanukkah lights. So some people think it is in memory of this that Christians first decorated their trees with candles and colored lights. A charming legend tells that on the cold winter night when Christ was born, all the trees in the forest miraculously burst into bloom and bore fruit. This may explain why we adorn our

Christmas trees with glass fruits and other shining ornaments.

Candles are used in other ways, too, at Christmas. In the Middle Ages, people put lighted candles in their windows to guide the Christ Child on His way, hoping He would come to their door. This is still done in France, Italy, Spain, and many other countries. Russians and Greeks receive lighted candles in church on Christmas Eve, which they celebrate on January 6. Many people hang Advent wreaths in their homes, with four candles, one of which is lighted each week during the period from December 6 until Christmas.

The flames of the Yule log also provide light. The custom of burning the Yule log comes originally from the medieval Scandinavian church, which ordered the "sacred log" to be burned as a symbolic destruction of ancient pagan beliefs. By now, the Yule log has acquired a new set of beliefs and superstitions, mostly secular in nature. A piece of one year's log is usually kept to light the fire of the next Yule log the following Christmas. This is said to bring good luck to the household for the year to come. (The Yule log may also be found on the dinner table, especially in France, in the form of a delectable log-shaped cake, called the *bûche de Noël*.)

The Druids burned a Yule log, too—usually one from an oak or apple tree. They also burned candles and hung mistletoe on tree

branches. From them came our pleasant Christmastime custom of hanging mistletoe above the doorway and kissing any guest who steps under it. "Decking the halls" with evergreens, a feature of the Roman Saturnalia, also has survived as a part of the Christmas tradition. Bringing in the beauty of the outdoors with holly and ivy, with evergreens and mistletoe, and, above all, with the Christmas tree, is an essential element of the holiday season.

AT CHRISTMAS TIME

English, Traditional

At Christmas time we deck the hall
With holly branches brave and tall,
With sturdy pine and hemlock bright
And in the Yule log's dancing light
We tell old tales of field and fight
    At Christmas time.

At Christmas time we pile the board
With flesh and fruit and vintage stored,
And mid the laughter and the glow
We tread a measure soft and slow,
And kiss beneath the mistletoe
    At Christmas time.

O CHRISTMAS TREE

GERMAN

Moderately

1. O Christ-mas Tree, O Christ-mas Tree, How true you stand un-chang-ing, O

Christ-mas Tree, O Christ-mas Tree, How true you stand un-chang-ing, Your

boughs so green in sum-mer-time, Re-main so green in win-ter-time O

Christ-mas Tree, O Christ-mas Tree, How true you stand un-chang-ing!

2. O Christmas Tree, O Christmas Tree,
   Thy message is enduring;
   O Christmas Tree, O Christmas Tree,
   Thy message is enduring;
   So long ago in Bethlehem
   Was born the Saviour of all men;
   O Christmas Tree, O Christmas Tree,
   Thy message is enduring.

3. O Christmas Tree, O Christmas Tree,
   Thy faith is so unchanging;
   O Christmas Tree, O Christmas Tree,
   Thy faith is so unchanging;
   A symbol sent from God above,
   Proclaiming Him the Lord of Love;
   O Christmas Tree, O Christmas Tree,
   How true you stand unchanging!

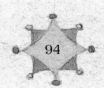

94

DECK THE HALLS

TRADITIONAL

OLD WELSH AIR

Deck the hall with boughs of hol - ly, Fa la la la la, la la la la.

'Tis the sea - son to be jol - ly, Fa la la la la, la la la la.

Don we now our gay ap-par - el, Fa la la la la la la,

Troll the an - cient Yule-tide car - ol, Fa, la, la, la, la, la, la, la, la.

2. See the blazing Yule before us,
Fa la la la la, la la la la.
Strike the harp and join the chorus,
Fa la la la la, la la la la.
Follow me in merry measure,
Fa la la la la la la,
While I tell of Yuletide treasure,
Fa, la, la, la, la, la, la, la, la.

3. Fast away the old year passes,
Fa la la la la, la la la la.
Hail the new, ye lads and lasses,
Fa la la la la, la la la la.
Sing we joyous all together,
Fa la la la la la la,
Heedless of the wind and weather,
Fa, la, la, la, la, la, la, la, la.

little tree

by e. e. cummings

little tree
little silent Christmas tree
you are so little
you are more like a flower

who found you in the green forest
and were you very sorry to come away?
see   i will comfort you
because you smell so sweetly

i will kiss your cool bark
and hug you safe and tight
just as your mother would,
only don't be afraid

look   the spangles

that sleep all the year in a dark box

dreaming of being taken out and allowed to shine,

the balls the chains red and gold the fluffy threads,

put up your little arms

and i'll give them all to you to hold

every finger shall have its ring

and there won't be a single place dark or unhappy

then when you're quite dressed

you'll stand in the window for everyone to see

and how they'll stare!

oh but you'll be very proud

and my little sister and i will take hands

and looking up at our beautiful tree

we'll dance and sing

"Noel Noel"

T H E   F I R   T R E E

by Hans Christian Andersen

Out in the wood was a fir tree, such a pretty little fir tree. It had a good place to grow in and all the air and sunshine it wanted, while all around it were numbers of bigger comrades, both firs and pines. But the little fir tree was in such a passionate hurry to grow. It paid no heed to the warmth of the sun or the sweetness of the air, and it took no notice of the village children who went chattering along when they were out after strawberries or raspberries; sometimes they came there with a whole jugful or had strawberries threaded on a straw, and then they sat down by the little tree and said, "Oh, what a dear little tree!" That was not at all the kind of thing the tree wanted to hear. . . .

"Oh, if only I were a tall tree like the others," sighed the little fir. "Then I'd be able to spread out my branches all 'round me and see out over the wide world with my top. The birds would come and nest in my branches and, whenever it was windy, I'd be able to nod grandly."

It took no pleasure in the sunshine or the birds or the pink clouds that, morning and evening, went sailing overhead.

When winter came and the snow lay sparkling white all around, then a hare would often come bounding along and jump right over the little tree—oh, how annoying that was! . . . But two winters passed and by the third winter the tree had grown so tall that the hare had to run around it.

Yes, grow, grow, become tall and old—that was much the finest thing in the world, thought the tree. . . .

"Rejoice in your youth," said the sunbeams, "rejoice in your lusty growth, and in the young life that is in you." And the wind kissed the tree, and the dew wept tears over it, but this meant nothing to the fir tree.

As Christmas drew near, quite young trees were cut down, trees that often were nothing like so big or so old as our fir tree, which knew no peace and was always longing to get away. These young trees—and they were just the very handsomest ones—

always kept their branches; they were laid on wagons and carted away by horses out of the wood.

"Where are they off to?" asked the fir tree. "They are no bigger than I am; there was even one that was much smaller. Why did they all keep their branches? Where are they going?"

"We know, we know!" twittered the sparrows. "We've been peeping in at the windows down in the town; we know where they're going. All the glory and splendor you can imagine awaits them. We looked in through the windowpanes and saw how the trees were planted in the middle of a cozy room and decorated with the loveliest things: gilded apples, honey cakes, toys, and hundreds of candles."

"And then?" asked the fir tree, quivering in every branch. "And then? What happens then?"

"Well, we didn't see any more. But it was magnificent."

"I wonder if it will be my fate to go that dazzling road," cried the tree in delight. "It's even better than crossing the ocean. How I'm longing for Christmas! I'm now just as tall and spreading as the others who were taken away last year. . . .

"Rejoice in me," said the air and the sunlight; "rejoice in your lusty youth out here in the open."

But the fir tree did nothing of the kind. It went on growing

and growing, there it was, winter and summer, always green—dark green. People who saw it remarked, "That's a pretty tree." And at the next Christmastime it was the first to be felled. The axe cut deep through pith and marrow, and the tree fell to the earth with a sigh, faint with pain, with no more thoughts of any happiness; it was so sad at parting from its home, from the place where it had grown up. For it knew that never again would it see those dear old friends, the little bushes and flowers that grew around—yes, and perhaps not even the birds. There was nothing pleasant about such a parting.

The tree didn't come to itself till it was being unloaded in the yard with the other trees and it heard a man say, "That one's a beauty—that's the one we'll have."

Now came two lackeys in full fig and carried the fir tree into a splendid great room. There were portraits all 'round on the walls, and by the big tile fireplace stood huge Chinese vases with lions on their lids. There were rocking-chairs, silk-covered sofas, large tables piled with picture books, and toys worth hundreds of dollars—at least, so said the children. And the fir tree was propped up in a great wooden barrel filled with sand, though no one could see it was a barrel because it was draped 'round with green cloth and was standing on a gay colored carpet. How the

tree trembled! Whatever was going to happen? Servants and young ladies alike were soon busy decorating it. On the branches they hung the little nets that had been cut out of colored paper, each net being filled with sweets; gilded apples and walnuts hung down as if they were growing there, and over a hundred red, blue, and white candles were fastened to the branches. Dolls that looked just like living people—such as the tree had never seen before—hovered among the greenery, while right up at the very top they had put a great star of gold tinsel; it was magnificent— you never saw anything like it.

"Tonight," they all said, "tonight it's going to sparkle—you'll see!"

"Oh, if only tonight were here!" thought the tree. "If only the candles were already lighted! What happens then, I wonder?"

At last the candles were lighted—what a blaze, what magnificence! It made the tree tremble in every branch . . . Then suddenly both folding doors flew open, and a flock of children came tearing in, as if they were going to upset the whole tree. The older people followed soberly behind; the little ones stood quite silent—but only for a moment—then they made the air ring with their shouts of delight. They danced 'round the tree, and one present after another was pulled off it.

"Whatever are they doing?" thought the tree. "What's going to happen?"

The children danced around with their splendid toys, and nobody looked at the tree except the old nurse, who went peering among the branches—though this was only to see if there wasn't some fig or apple that had been overlooked.

"A story—tell us a story!" cried the children, dragging a little fat man over towards the tree. He sat down right under it, "for then we are in the greenwood," he said, "and it will be so good for the tree to listen with you."

The little fat man told them the story of Humpty-Dumpty, who fell downstairs and yet came to the throne and married the Princess. And the children clapped their hands and called out, "Tell us another story! One more!" They wanted to have Hickory-Dickory as well, but they only got the one about Humpty-Dumpty. The fir tree stood there in silent thought; never had the birds out in the wood told a story like that. "Humpty-Dumpty fell downstairs and yet married the Princess—well, well, that's how they go on in the great world!" thought the fir tree, . . .

"Well, who knows? Maybe I too shall fall downstairs and marry a Princess."

The next morning in came a manservant and a maid. "Now

all the doings will begin again," thought the tree. Instead, they hauled it out of the room, up the stairs and into the attic, where they stowed it away in a dark corner out of the daylight. "What's the meaning of this?" wondered the tree. "What is there for me to do here? What am I to listen to?" And it leaned up against the wall and stood there thinking and thinking . . . It had plenty of time for that, because days and nights went by.

"It's winter by now outside," thought the tree. "The ground will be hard and covered with snow, people wouldn't be able to plant me; so I expect I shall have to shelter here till the spring. How considerate! How kind people are! . . . If only it weren't so dark and so terribly lonely in here! Not even a little hare . . . It was so jolly out in the wood, when the snow was lying and the hare went bounding past; yes, even when it jumped right over me, though I didn't like it at the time. Now that's over too . . . though I shall remember to enjoy myself, when I'm taken out again."

But when would that happen? Well, it happened one morning when people came up and rummaged about the attic. The boxes were being moved, and the tree was dragged out. They certainly dumped it rather hard onto the floor, but one of the men at once pulled it along towards the stairs where there was daylight.

"Life's beginning again for me!" thought the tree. It could feel

the fresh air, the first sunbeams—and now it was out in the courtyard. Everything happened so quickly that the tree quite forgot to look at itself, there was so much to see all around. The yard gave onto a garden where everything was in bloom. The roses smelled so sweet and fresh as they hung over the little trellis, and the lime trees were blossoming, . . .

"This is the life for me!" the fir tree cried out joyfully, spreading out its branches. Alas! They were all withered and yellow, and the tree lay in a corner among weeds and nettles. The gold paper star was still in its place at the top and glittered away in the bright sunshine.

Playing in the courtyard itself were a few of the merry children who at Christmastime had danced 'round the tree and were so pleased with it. One of the smallest ran up and tore off the gold star.

"Look what I've found still there on that nasty old Christmas tree!" he said, trampling on the branches so that they crackled under his boots.

And the tree looked at the fresh beauty of the flowers in the garden, and then at itself, and it wished it had stayed in that dark corner up in the attic. It thought of the fresh days of its youth in the wood, of that merry Christmas Eve, and of the little children

who had listened with such delight to the story of Humpty-Dumpty.

"All over!" said the poor tree, "if only I had been happy while I could! All over!" . . .

The boys were playing in the yard, and the smallest of them had on his chest the gold star which had crowned the tree on its happiest evening. That was all over now, and it was all over with the tree, and so it is with the story. That's what happens at last to every story—all over, all over!

{ Note: This story has been slightly abridged. }

FIR TREE TALL

by Joan Hanson

Fir
tree tall
Lights glittering
Bright tinsel hung
Shimmering, glimmering
Laughter shining in the eyes
Of boys
and girls
Lovely lovely
Christmas tree.

THE CHRISTMAS TREE

Excerpted from A CHRISTMAS MEMORY

by Truman Capote

The author, as a little boy, lived for a time in a small town in rural Alabama with a beloved elderly relative, Miss Sook Faulk, to whom he refers as his "friend" in this memoir. Here he tells of going with her and his dog, Queenie, to get the tree and other things to decorate the house for Christmas.

I know where we'll find real pretty trees, Buddy. And holly, too. With berries big as your eyes. It's way off in the woods. Farther than we've ever been. Papa used to bring us Christmas trees from there: carry them on his shoulder. That's fifty years ago. Well, now: I can't wait for morning."

Morning. Frozen rime lusters the grass; the sun, round as an orange and orange as hot-weather moons, balances on the horizon, burnishes the silvered winter woods. A wild turkey calls. A renegade hog grunts in the undergrowth. Soon, by the edge of knee-deep, rapid-running water, we have to abandon the buggy.

Queenie wades the stream first, paddles across barking complaints at the swiftness of the current, the pneumonia-making coldness of it. We follow, holding our shoes and equipment (a hatchet, a burlap sack) above our heads. A mile more: of chastising thorns, burs and briers that catch at our clothes; of rusty pine needles brilliant with gaudy fungus and molted feathers. Here, there, a flash, a flutter, an ecstasy of shrillings remind us that not all the birds have flown south. Always the path unwinds through lemony sun pools and pitch-black vine tunnels. Another creek to cross: a disturbed armada of speckled trout froths the water round us, and frogs the size of plates practice belly flops; beaver workmen are building a dam. On the farther shore, Queenie shakes herself and trembles. My friend shivers, too: not with cold but enthusiasm. One of her hat's ragged roses sheds a petal as she lifts her head and inhales the pine-heavy air. "We're almost there; can you smell it, Buddy?" she says, as though we were approaching an ocean.

And, indeed, it is a kind of ocean. Scented acres of holiday trees, prickly-leafed holly. Red berries shiny as Chinese bells: black crows swoop upon them screaming. Having stuffed our burlap sacks with enough greenery and crimson to garland a dozen windows, we set about choosing a tree. "It should be,"

muses my friend, "twice as tall as a boy. So a boy can't steal the star." The one we pick is twice as tall as me. A brave handsome brute that survives thirty hatchet strokes before it keels with a creaking, rending cry. Lugging it like a kill, we commence the long trek out. Every few yards we abandon the struggle, sit down and pant. But we have the strength of triumphant huntsmen; that and the tree's virile, icy perfume revive us, goad us on. Many compliments accompany our sunset return along the red clay road to town; but my friend is sly and noncommittal when passers-by praise the treasure perched in our buggy: what a fine tree and where did it come from? "Yonderways," she murmurs vaguely. Once a car stops and the rich mill owner's lazy wife leans out and whines: "Giveya two-bits cash for that ol tree." Ordinarily my friend is afraid of saying no; but on this occasion she promptly shakes her head: "We wouldn't take a dollar." The mill owner's wife persists. "A dollar, my foot! Fifty cents. That's my last offer. Goodness, woman, you can get another one." In answer, my friend gently reflects: "I doubt it. There's never two of anything."

Home: Queenie slumps by the fire and sleeps till tomorrow, snoring loud as a human.

A trunk in the attic contains: a shoebox of ermine tails (off

the opera cape of a curious lady who once rented a room in the house), coils of frazzled tinsel gone gold with age, one silver star, a brief rope of dilapidated, undoubtedly dangerous candy-like light bulbs. Excellent decorations, as far as they go, which isn't far enough: my friend wants our tree to blaze "like a Baptist window," droop with weighty snows of ornament. But we can't afford the made-in-Japan splendors at the five-and-dime. So we do what we've always done: sit for days at the kitchen table with scissors and crayons and stacks of colored paper. I make sketches and my friend cuts them out: lots of cats, fish too (because they're easy to draw), some apples, some watermelons, a few winged angels devised from saved-up sheets of Hershey-bar tin foil. We use safety pins to attach these creations to the tree; as a final touch, we sprinkle the branches with shredded cotton (picked in August for this purpose). My friend, surveying the effect, clasps her hands together. "Now honest, Buddy. Doesn't it look good enough to eat?" Queenie tries to eat an angel.

CHRISTMAS IN THE WOODS

Excerpted from the book THE FAIRY CARAVAN

by Beatrix Potter

In the night before Christmas Eve there came a fall of snow. Down below in the glen the waters of the stream tinkled through the ground ice. Now and then there was a soft rushing sound as the wet snow slipped off the sapling trees that bent beneath its weight and sprang upward again, released.

Far off in the woods a branch snapped under its load, like the sound of a gun at night. The stream murmured, flowing darkly. Dead keshes (withered grass) and canes stood up through the snow on its banks under a fringe of hazel bushes.

Between the stream and the tree there was a white untrodden slope. Only one tree grew there, a very small spruce, a little

Christmas tree some four feet high. As the night grew darker the branches of this little tree became all tipped with light and wreathed with icicles and chains of frost. Brighter and brighter it shone, until it seemed to bear a hundred fairy lights, not like the yellow gleam of candles but a clear, white incandescent light.

Small voices and music began to mingle with the sound of the water. Up the snowy banks, from the wood and from the meadow beyond, tripped scores of little shadowy creatures advancing from the darkness into the light.

They trod a circle on the snow around the Christmas tree, dancing gaily hand in hand. Rabbits, moles, squirrels, and wood mice danced hand in paw with a wood mouse and a shrew— while a hedgehog played the bagpipes beneath the fairy spruce.

CHRISTMAS
EVERYWHERE

CHRISTMAS EVERYWHERE

"Joy to the world!" exclaims the familiar carol, and indeed there are few parts of the globe today where one cannot find Christians celebrating the birth of Jesus. Customs and traditions may differ from one country to another, but the spiritual essence is universal. Symbols of Christmas such as the star and the tree and traditions such as gift giving and the setting up of "mangers" or nativity scenes characterize celebrations everywhere. Children the world over sing, take part in holiday processions, or act in Christmas plays and pageants. Church services follow tradition, but the secular festivities, whether gala or solemn, vary widely.

In some parts of the world, the Holy Family is envisioned as

resembling the local inhabitants; for example, they may be light-skinned or dark, or have Asian or Polynesian features. This is natural: all of us are most comfortable with what is most familiar to us, and these transformations do not vitiate the power of the spiritual essence, the story of the birth of Christ. (An Indonesian Christian woman recalls that in the nativity pageants of her childhood, the members of the Holy Family could believably be represented by children with black hair, but there were very few angels, as there were almost no children in the community with the long blond hair that was then considered requisite!)

While giving gifts at Christmastime is universal, the bringer of the gifts differs, as well as his or her costume and means of transportation. In Sydney, Australia, and halfway across the world in São Paulo, Brazil, Santa Claus emerges from the sea, clad in red bathing trunks but bearing his familiar sack of toys. Sometimes he even arrives on water skis! In parts of Africa where it is very hot, he may wear red shorts. In other countries he has evolved slightly differently but his character as bringer of gifts to children has become almost universal.

In the Scandinavian countries, the gift bringer is the Jultomten,

a kindly elf who looks a great deal like Santa Claus and who arrives on a sleigh drawn by reindeer or sometimes a goat. He traces his ancestry, however, not to Saint Nicholas but to the Nordic god Thor and to the ancient celebration of Jul or Yule, when the sun began its return to Earth, and the days began to lengthen after the long, dark winter. The Russians' Grandfather Frost is probably also related to the celebration of the winter solstice, as he brings his gifts to children on New Year's Day rather than on Christmas Day. In Germany, gift giving is some-what more closely associated with the origin of Christmas, the nativity of Jesus, and it is the Christkindl, the Holy Child, who is the gift giver. Early German settlers brought the name to the United States, where it came, over the years, to be pronounced Kriss Kringle. The gift giver's personality changed, too, and took on many of the characteristics of Santa Claus. Now the two are almost interchangeable. But Saint Nicholas may also appear in Germany, wearing his red robe and riding on a white horse. Sometimes he is accompanied by the Christkindl. And he is often followed (or replaced) by the dreaded Knecht Ruprecht, who delivers gifts to the good but punishes the bad. Most French children leave their shoes for Père Noël to fill with gifts, in

exchange for an apple left for his horse. In Normandy, however, they leave their wooden sabots. This is the tradition in Holland, also, though it is Sinter Claes who is the gift bringer here, with his Moorish helper, Black Peter. In Indonesia, where apples are not grown, a carrot is left for Sinter Claes's horse instead.

Although local customs and secular celebrations of the joys of the season may differ, all are united in spirit by the message of the angels on the first Christmas: "Glory to God in the highest, and on earth peace, good will toward men."

AND THERE WERE IN THE SAME COUNTRY SHEPHERDS abiding in the field, keeping watch over their flock by night.

And, lo, the angel of the Lord came upon them, and the glory of the Lord shone round about them: and they were sore afraid.

And the angel said unto them, Fear not: for, behold, I bring you good tidings of great joy, which shall be to all people.

For unto you is born this day in the city of David a Saviour, which is Christ the Lord.

And this shall be a sign unto you; Ye shall find the babe wrapped in swaddling clothes, lying in a manger.

And suddenly there was with the angel a multitude of the heavenly host praising God, and saying,

Glory to God in the highest, and on earth peace, good will toward men.

Luke 2:8–14

JOY TO THE WORLD!

Isaac Watts

Georg Friedrich Händel

Majestically

1. Joy to the world! the Lord is come; Let earth re-ceive her King; Let ev-'ry heart pre-pare Him room, And heav'n and na-ture sing, And heav'n and na-ture sing, And heav-en and heav-en and na-ture sing.

2. Joy to the world! the Saviour reigns;
   Let men their songs employ;
   While fields and floods, rocks, hills and plains
   Repeat the sounding joy,
   Repeat the sounding joy,
   Repeat, repeat the sounding joy.

3. He rules the world with truth and grace,
   And makes the nations prove
   The glories of His righteousness,
   And wonders of His love,
   And wonders of His love,
   And wonders, and wonders of His Love.

125

HARK! THE HERALD ANGELS SING

CHARLES WESLEY, 1739

FELIX MENDELSSOHN, 1840

Hark! the her-ald an-gels sing,_ "Glor-y to_ the new-born King! Peace on earth, and mer-cy mild,_ God and sin-ners re-con-ciled." Joy-ful, all ye na-tions, rise,_ Join the tri-umph of the skies;_ With th'an-gel-ic host pro-claim, "Christ is_ born in Beth-le-hem." Hark! the her-ald an-gels sing, "Glor-y to the new-born King!"

2. Christ, by highest heav'n adored;
Christ, the everlasting Lord;
Late in time behold Him come,
Offspring of the favored one.
Veiled in flesh, the Godhead see;
Hail th'incarnate Deity
Pleased, as man with men to dwell,
Jesus, our Immanuel!
Hark! the herald angels sing,
"Glory to the new-born King!"

3. Hail! the heav'n-born Prince of Peace!
Hail! the Son of Righteousness!
Light and life to all He brings,
Ris'n with healing in His wings.
Mild He lays His glory by,
Born that man no more may die;
Born to raise the sons of earth,
Born to give them second birth.
Hark! the herald angels sing,
"Glory to the new-born King!"

GRANDFATHER FROST, THE TSAR OF WINTER

by Nikolai A. Nekrasov

*"Winter is a shining, luminescent joy in the soul of every Russian,"
according to Nikolai Nekrasov, whose rhapsodic poem written
in 1863 about the joys of the snowy season and the celebration
of Christmas in that country is known by adults and children
alike. Here is a prose translation of an excerpt from the beloved
longer poem.*

The Tsar of Winter, who is also known as Grandfather
Frost, is the ruler of a vast and beautiful country! When
he harnesses his swift white-winged horses, they carry him in
his sleigh high above the fields and forests. He looks down to
make sure that every field and every tree in the forest is
clothed in magnificent garments of snow. He watches to see
that every river and every little brook is frozen solidly into a
shining chain of ice.

The Tsar of Winter is a very powerful ruler. Everything is subject to him: blizzards, snowstorms, icy winds. All of nature trembles, when he sings his harsh songs.

The Tsar of Winter's realm is enormous! It stretches from the great European plain to Siberia, far in the north, and westward from the Pacific Ocean all the way to the North Sea . . . a tremendous expanse. The name of this great land is Russia.

Like all the Tsars who have ever existed, Grandfather Frost is sometimes capricious, or even malicious. But most of the time he is kind and generous. He covers his whole land with a huge white fur coat. He paints magnificent patterns on the windows of houses. He hangs beautiful lace garlands on the trees: firs, birches, oaks, and maples.

He makes Russian churches and monasteries look even more majestic—truly sublime, adding a pearly sheen to their golden domes.

Grandfather Frost gives his people countless generous gifts. He may craft a small sledding hill for children, or change a river

into an icy speedway for merchants. Everything is a joy for
him. Like a child himself, Grandfather Frost enjoys the games
children play in the snow. He slides down the hills with them,
breathless with excitement. Even if someone falls off the sled,
there are no tears, as the snow-white rug is soft and furry.
Laughter and happiness reign here.

Troikas fly along rivers that have miraculously become roads; the
coachmen sing their lively songs, giving thanks to Grandfather
Frost. Grandfather Frost enjoys it all. He playfully pinches
people's noses and reddens their cheeks. Where the ground is too
icy, he sprinkles a light covering of snow on it so that travelers
can ride their horses faster.

Now people hasten to visit neighboring towns and villages. Some
want to visit friends, some have business to do, and all of them
admire how the earth has magically changed with the snow. All
the familiar places have become wonderfully transformed.

Grandfather Frost, the magician of winter, is very pleased that
his artwork touches people's hearts. For his art is great and
eternal; his glorious and priceless gift is beauty. He offers it

freely to all: to children and adults alike, in abundance, gladdening the eye and bringing peace to the spirit. In the soul of every Russian, winter is a shining, luminescent joy.

The sonorous ringing of bells sounds all over the snowcovered land of Russia. The chiming of the bells can be heard from one village to another. It announces one of the greatest holidays of all—Christmas.

All over Russia in every church, large or small, there are holiday services. Christmas Eve is very solemn and quiet. At this holy time, Grandfather Frost lets his horses rest. He himself pays tribute and honors the Creator.

The next morning a different kind of holiday begins. This is truly a merry Christmas, celebrated with songs and traditional round dances.

All over great Russia there is rejoicing. People make merry in the open air. Songs ring out as troikas race on the frozen rivers. Children dance around the Christmas tree, calling for

Grandfather Frost to come. People wander from house to house, where they are given sweets and gifts left for them by Grandfather Frost. Grandfather Frost sees all this and is glad that the children are happy. And he is glad that on this great and glorious holiday his land is clad in beauty, thanks to his efforts.

Where beauty is, there is love! Where love is, there is God!

"Glory to God in the highest, and on earth peace, good will toward men."

THE TAILOR OF GLOUCESTER

A CHRISTMAS PLAY, BASED ON THE BOOK

by Beatrix Potter

This delightful adaptation of the book was proposed to Beatrix Potter by Mr. E. Harcourt Williams, who sent her a rough draft of a play he had written for a children's Christmastime performance. Ms. Potter was charmed by this proposal but made so many changes and corrections to Williams's text that, when her editors at Frederick Warne asked her to rewrite it for publication in book form, she replied, "Between ourselves the present version is so far mine (by quotation and corrections) that I could not write a different version if I tried." It was published in 1930, the first of several plays to be adapted by Potter or others from her popular books.

Characters

 The Tailor

 Andrew, a Mouse

 Dame Simpkin, His Housekeeper, a Cat

 Pippin, a Mouse

 The Mayor of Gloucester

 Gammon, a Mouse

 Spinach, A Mouse

TIME: *A Christmas Eve in the 18th century*

SETTING: *The Tailor's house in College Court, London*

AT RISE: *Christmas carols can be heard being sung in the street outside. The Tailor is seen working at his table.*

TAILOR: This is the finest coat that ever I made and the waist-coat is bravely cut out. There is naught now to finish except the button holes, with cherry coloured twisted silk. But I have no more twist (*looking towards window*)—How it snows! Alas my poor rheumatic bones! (*rubs his knees*) Dame Simpkin must fetch it for me from the silk mercer's. See there is no stuff cut to waste (*holding up little pieces*). No more than will make waistcoats for mice! Ribbons for mob caps for mice! (*Calls*) Simpkin, Dame Simpkin!

Enter Dame Simpkin. 'Miaw, miaw'.

Yes, I know it snows. But we are going to make our fortunes. His worship the mayor of Gloucester is to be married on Christmas day in the morning and he hath ordered a coat and an embroidered waistcoat.

SIMPKIN: Miaw, miaw.

TAILOR: This is Christmas Eve and I must hurry, Dame Simp-kin, I must hurry. I wish I had more time for the work even though there are only the button holes. How the snow keeps falling! It is very cold tonight, Simpkin. Don't you think we might have a dish of tay to cheer our hearts?

SIMPKIN: G r r r Miaw (*puts kettle on hob*).

TAILOR: Dame Simpkin don't be cross. I do so want a dish of tay, my rheumatics are bad, very bad. I have four pennies left; you will find them in the tea pot on the dresser. Simpkin, do be kind and good; and brew the tay before you go.

SIMPKIN: (*less cross*) Miaw, miaw.

TAILOR: Aye, Simpkin, good Simpkin; you would talk if you could. Well, well, who knows? Old men talking to themselves—old men, old times, old tales. What said the old story?—that all animals can talk in the night between Christmas Eve, and Christmas day in the morning. But only the kind hearts can hear them, and know what it is that they say.

SIMPKIN: (*showing empty trencher*) Miaw, miaw!

TAILOR: What? Have the little mice eaten our last crumb of bread?

SIMPKIN: (*looking about*) Miaw, miaw!

TAILOR: No, no, Dame Simpkin. The little things must eat. They mean no harm. And how clever and nimble; never cross or rheumatic. Why, behind the walls of this old house there are little mouse staircases—little secret trap doors and the mice scamper through long narrow passages from house to house. They can run all over the town without going out into the streets.

SIMPKIN: Miaw.

TAILOR: Don't be a cruel cross-patch, Dame Simpkin. You mustn't sniff at mouse holes and whisk your wicked tail. Now take the china pipkin and buy a penn'orth of bread, a penn'orth of milk—and a penn'orth of sausage. And oh, Simpkin, with the last penny of our fourpence buy me one penn'orth of cherry coloured silk. But do not lose the last penny of my fourpence or I shall be undone and worn to a ravelling for I have no more twist.

SIMPKIN: (*Taking money and pipkin.*) Miaw!

TAILOR: Poor Simpkin, I know you hate the snow, but I must have that twisted silk.

(*There is a knock at outer door. Dame Simpkin opens and the Mayor enters. With a last plaintive miaw Dame Simpkin goes out closing the door behind her*).

MAYOR: (*pompously*) Now, Master Tailor, is my cherry coloured coat and embroidered waistcoat ready?

TAILOR: Oh, your worship must give me until tomorrow. There's a deal of work in a cherry coloured corded silk coat embroidered with pansies and roses—not to mention a cream coloured satin waistcoat trimmed with gauze and green worsted chenille.

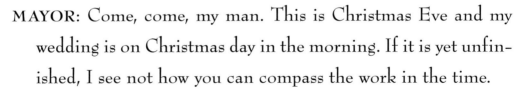
MAYOR: Come, come, my man. This is Christmas Eve and my wedding is on Christmas day in the morning. If it is yet unfinished, I see not how you can compass the work in the time.

TAILOR: It shall be ready, your worship. It shall be ready. I give you my word.

MAYOR: The word of a tailor, indeed! If you fail me (*at the door*) you shall eat your plum pudding in the stocks tomorrow, Christmas day or no Christmas day.

(*The Mayor goes out. The Carol singers pass again, a clock strikes twelve.*)

TAILOR: Alack I am undone. I am worn to a ravelling. I have no more strength and no time—where is Simpkin with that twist—(*sinks into chair*)—Oh dear, oh dear,—the waistcoat to be lined with taffeta—and the taffeta sufficeth—there is no more left over in snippets than will serve to make tippets for mice—(*there is a tapping noise*) now what can that be? This is very peculiar. Ah, naughty Simpkin, has she set the mouse trap?—Poor little frightened thing, I'll let you out.

(*Pippin steps out and curtsies.*)

PIPPIN: Mistress Pippin at your service

TAILOR: (*bowing*) I wish you a merry Christmas, Ma'am (*goes back to chair*). Queer. I must be dreaming—I have an idea that

mouse said something—the waistcoat is cut from peach coloured satin—tambour stitch and rosebuds in beautiful floss silk—was I wise to entrust my last fourpence to Simpkin—but we shall be rich if all is ready for his worship in the morning—I must go on working . . . one and twenty button-holes of cherry coloured twist.

(*Tapping noise again*)

This is passing extraordinary—there must have been two mice in the trap (*opens it—Andrew steps out and bows*).

ANDREW: Master Andrew at your service.

TAILOR: (*bowing*) Your humble servant, Sir, and I wish you the compliments of the season (*back to chair*). Odd, very odd. One and twenty button-holes of cherry coloured silk—to be finished by Christmas morning—and it is after midnight already—was I right to let out those mice? Undoubtedly they belonged to Dame Simpkin. Alack I am undone for I have no more twist—no more twist—(*he falls asleep*).

ANDREW: Where are Gammon and Spinach?

PIPPIN: Here they are. I had to send them back for thimbles; the Tailor's were too big.

GAMMON: Oh, poor old tailor!

ANDREW: I fear he is very ill.

PIPPIN: La! how pale he looks.

ANDREW: Let us finish the coat and waistcoat for him, then the joyful surprise will make him well again.

SPINACH: (*looking at the clothes*) Are they not truly elegant?

GAMMON: Delicious!

ANDREW: Come now, to work, to work, and meanwhile do you, Master Spinach, give us a tune on your fiddle.

PIPPIN: First let us bar the door in case naughty Simpkin comes back.

ANDREW: Well said, Mistress Pippin (*he bars the door*).

GAMMON: These needles are very large, though easy to thread. (*They have mounted the table and begin business of threading needles and stitching. They sing.*)

> Four-and-twenty tailors
> Went to catch a snail,
> The best man amongst them
> Durst not touch her tail;
> She put out her horns
> Like a little kyloe cow,
> Run, tailors, run! or she'll have you all
> e'en now!

(Dame Simpkin opens the grill in the door and pushes her face through.)

SIMPKIN: Miaw!

GAMMON: *(laughing)* No, no, the door is barred; you can't get in.

SPINACH: *(laughing)* Hey diddle diddle, the cat and the fiddle!

SIMPKIN: What a charming sight. Please unfasten the door.

PIPPIN: No thank you, Dame Simpkin, we don't want to be baked in your Christmas mince pies.

SPINACH: Three little mice sat down to spin.

GAMMON: Pussy passed by and she peeped in.

SIMPKIN: What are you at, my fine little men?

GAMMON: Making coats for gentlemen.

SIMPKIN: Shall I come in and cut off your threads?

SPINACH: Oh no, Miss Pussy, you'll bite off our heads.

SIMPKIN: Once upon a time a cat and mouse kept house together—

ANDREW: Thank you, we have heard that story—May I trouble you for the scissors, M'am?

PIPPIN: More twist please—

GAMMON: Why there is no more twist.

PIPPIN: No more twist?

ALL: No more twist!

SIMPKIN: Ah ha, I have the twist. I have been out to buy it—So now you must let me in.

PIPPIN: No, no, you will gobble us up, Dame Simpkin.

SIMPKIN: No, I give you my word.

PIPPIN: Your word?

SIMPKIN: Indeed I won't eat you.

SPINACH: I don't think a cat's word is to be trusted.

SIMPKIN: But I promise.

ANDREW: Promise. Oh very well then. But you must sit at the other end of the kitchen.

PIPPIN: And you mustn't wave your tail.

(They open the door.)

SIMPKIN: *(purring)* Oh I am glad to come in. It is very cold outside and my coat is quite wet with snow, and you know how cats hate that *(puts milk and bread down)*. I have been thinking—this is Christmas day, so I won't be a cruel old cat any more—and you kind little mice have been helping my poor tired old master! So here is the cherry coloured twist—

ANDREW: Quick, quick! To work, to work! Time is flying. *(A rapid song 'Nick-nack paddywack.' During the singing the light*

144

fades out leaving only the one candle by which they work. The voices become very soft. The Tailor snores. Then in the distance is heard the cry of the watchman. 'Eight o'clock and a fine frosty morning!'

ANDREW: Away, away!

(*They scamper about clearing up. The Christmas bells ring out. A loud knocking at the door.*)

SIMPKIN: Who can that be?

GAMMON: Ready?

SPINACH: All ready.

ALL: Away! (*The mice vanish. Dame Simpkin opens door. Enter the Mayor.*)

MAYOR: Now then, Madam, where is your Master?

(*Dame Simpkin gently paws the tailor.*)

TAILOR: (*waking up*) Eh? eh? One and twenty button-holes, I am undone.

MAYOR: How now, Master Tailor, are my coat and waistcoat finished?

TAILOR: Oh, forgive me, your Worship. Alas, I fell asleep.

MAYOR: Fell asleep, you villain—you breaker of words? Do you mean to tell me they are not completed?

TAILOR: Oh, I shall be ruined. Oh, Simpkin, Simpkin, if only you had brought me that cherry coloured silk twist.

MAYOR: Twist, indeed. I'll twist you!

(*Dame Simpkin jumps on table and makes violent signs.*)

MAYOR: Ho there! I will call the watch.

TAILOR: What is it, Simpkin? (*seeing finished clothes*) Oh, how can it be—look they are finished, and what beautiful work, every button-hole.

MAYOR: Neat, very neat, I wonder how they could be stitched by an old man in spectacles with old crooked fingers and a tailor's thimble.

TAILOR: (*peering at work*) Yes, your Worship, the stitches are uncommonly small, so small, one might almost think that they had been worked by little mice.

SIMPKIN: (*dancing on trap*) Miaw!

MAYOR: But that's preposterous!

TAILOR: Simpkin, was it really the mice? How very very kind of them. We won't set traps again, will we, good Simpkin?

SIMPKIN: (*repentant*) Miaw!

MAYOR: I think you have both gone crazy.

TAYLOR: Here, your Worship, is your suit and may it bring you great happiness in your married life.

MAYOR: I thank you, Master Tailor. It is indeed well done. I shall recommend you to my friends, and here is the gold I promised you with a little more besides because it is Christmas morning.

TAILOR: I thank you, Sir, for your graciousness. Dame Simpkin, will you please open the door for his Worshipfulness?

TAILOR: Simpkin, we have made our fortune. The Mayor will recommend us to his friends. Come give me my hat and my cloak. I feel a new man. Do put on your bonnet. We'll go shopping. You shall have cream for breakfast. The little children next door shall have some toys. We'll have a Christmas goose and plum pudding for dinner, and the mice shall have some toasted cheese! (*They open the door, a carol greets their ears*)

CURTAIN

THE TWELVE DAYS OF CHRISTMAS

OLD ENGLISH OR SCOTTISH AIR

On the first day of Christ - mas My

true love sent to me, A par - tridge _ in a pear tree. On the

sec - ond day of Christ - mas My true love sent to me,

Two tur - tle doves, and a par - tridge _ in a pear

Repeat through no. 12, adding one line each repetition.

sixth day of Christ – mas My true love sent to me
seventh day etc. . .

6. Six geese a – lay – ing,
7. Seven swans a – swim – ming,
8. Eight maids a – milk – ing,
9. Nine la – dies danc – ing, Five gold rings,
10. Ten lords a – leap – ing,
11. Eleven pip – ers pip – ing,
12. Twelve drum – mers drum – ming,

four call – ing birds, three French hens, two tur – tle doves, and a

Through 11th day repeat. | *Final ending after 12th day.*

par – tridge in a pear tree. On the tree.

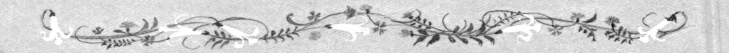

THE CRATCHITS' CHRISTMAS DINNER

From A CHRISTMAS CAROL

by Charles Dickens

Readings and dramatizations of this sentimental but satisfying tale have become a traditional part of the Christmas scene in every English-speaking part of the globe. It was written in 1843, when Dickens was just thirty-one years old. The first edition of this book sold out on the first day of publication and brought its young author both critical acclaim and popular success. The story tells of the conversion of Ebenezer Scrooge from a hardhearted miser into a generous, affectionate, and happy man. "Bah! Humbug!" is Scrooge's reply when his nephew wishes him a Merry Christmas. But that night, Christmas Eve, Scrooge is confronted by the ghost of his dead partner Marley and the spirits of Christmases Past, Present, and Yet to Come. The spirits show Scrooge what sorrow the future holds for him unless he changes his unkind ways. By contrast, they also show him scenes of poor but happy families celebrating Christmas together with a joy and warmth that he, too, might share if he would only open his heart. A favorite part of the story is the description of the family of Bob Cratchit, Scrooge's underpaid assistant, at their frugal but nonetheless festive Christmas dinner:

His active little crutch was heard upon the floor, and back came Tiny Tim before another word was spoken, escorted by his brother and sister to his stool before the fire; and while Bob, turning up his cuffs—as if, poor fellow, they were capable of being made more shabby—compounded some hot mixture in a jug with gin and lemons, and stirred it round and round and put it on the hob to simmer; Master Peter, and the two ubiquitous young Cratchits went to fetch the goose, with which they soon returned in high procession.

Such a bustle ensued that you might have thought a goose the rarest of all birds; a feathered phenomenon, to which a black swan was a matter of course—and in truth it was something very like it in that house. Mrs. Cratchit made the gravy (ready beforehand in a little saucepan) hissing hot; Master Peter mashed the potatoes with incredible vigor; Miss Belinda sweetened up the apple-sauce; Martha dusted the hot plates; Bob took Tiny Tim beside him in a tiny corner at the table; the two young Cratchits set chairs for everybody, not forgetting themselves, and mounting guard upon their posts, crammed spoons into their mouths, lest they should shriek for goose before their turn came to be helped. At last the dishes were set on, and grace was said. It was

succeeded by a breathless pause, as Mrs. Cratchit, looking slowly all along the carving-knife, prepared to plunge it in the breast, but when she did, and when the long-expected gush of stuffing issued forth, one murmur of delight arose all 'round the board, and even Tiny Tim, excited by the two young Cratchits, beat on the table with the handle of his knife, and feebly cried Hurrah!

There never was such a goose. Bob said he didn't believe there ever was such a goose cooked. Its tenderness and flavor, size and cheapness, were the themes of universal admiration. Eked out by apple-sauce and mashed potatoes, it was a sufficient dinner for the whole family; indeed, as Mrs. Cratchit said with great delight (surveying one small atom of a bone upon the dish), they hadn't ate it all at last! Yet everyone had had enough, and the youngest Cratchits in particular, were steeped in sage and onion to the eyebrows! But now, the plates being changed by Miss Belinda, Mrs. Cratchit left the room alone—too nervous to bear wit-ness—to take the pudding up and bring it in.

Suppose it should not be done enough! Suppose it should break in turning out! Suppose somebody should have got over the wall of the back-yard, and stolen it, while they were merry with

goose—a supposition at which the two young Cratchits became livid! All sorts of horrors were supposed.

Hallo! A great deal of steam! The pudding was out of the copper. A smell like a washing-day! That was the cloth. A smell like an eating-house and a pastrycook's next door to each other, with a laundress's next door to that! That was the pudding! In half a minute Mrs. Cratchit entered—flushed, but smiling proudly—with the pudding, like a speckled cannon-ball, so hard and firm, blazing in half of half-a-quartern of ignited brandy, and bedight with Christmas holly stuck into the top.

Oh, a wonderful pudding! Bob Cratchit said, and calmly too, that he regarded it as the greatest success achieved by Mrs. Cratchit since their marriage. Mrs. Cratchit said that now the weight was off her mind, she would confess she had had her doubts about the quantity of flour. Everybody had something to say about it, but nobody said or thought it was at all a small pudding for a large family. It would have been flat heresy to do so. Any Cratchit would have flushed to hint at such a thing.

At last the dinner was all done, the cloth was cleared, the hearth swept, and the fire made up. The compound in the jug being tasted, and considered perfect, apples and oranges were

put upon the table, and a shovelful of chestnuts on the fire. Then all the Cratchit family drew round the hearth, in what Bob Cratchit called a circle, meaning half a one; and at Bob Cratchit's elbow stood the family display of glass. Two tumblers, and a custard-cup without a handle.

These held the hot stuff from the jug, however, as well as golden goblets would have done; and Bob served it out with beaming looks, while the chestnuts on the fire sputtered and cracked noisily. Then Bob proposed:

"A Merry Christmas to all, my dears. God bless us!" Which all the family re-echoed.

"God bless us every one!" said Tiny Tim, the last of all.

AMAHL AND THE NIGHT VISITORS

Excerpted from the book AMAHL AND THE NIGHT VISITORS

by Gian-Carlo Menotti and Frances Frost

In the United States, Gian-Carlo Menotti's opera is a beloved fea-
ture of every Christmas season, in live performance or broadcast
on television and radio. Here, preserving the original dialogue of
the opera, poet Frances Frost tells the tender story of a small boy's
simple gift for the Christ Child and the miracle that followed.

Amahl, a little shepherd boy with a crippled leg, and his wid-
owed mother were startled when three kings knocked at the
door of their humble cottage and asked to stay the night. Amahl
and his mother welcomed the travelers. But they themselves were
desperately poor and they had no food at all to offer their royal
guests. Neighbors—shepherds and their families—came to their
rescue, bringing a simple but bountiful feast, and then . . .

The three kings watched with delight as a boy and a girl came
shyly to the middle of the floor and began a dance to entertain

the kings and show them welcome and hospitality. Gradually other dancers joined the first couple, and the music and the dance grew in pace and sureness. Amahl and the old shepherd piped faster and faster, till the dance ended in a joyous frenzy. Amahl and the old shepherd put down their pipes and smiled at each other, while the breathless dancers smiled and bowed to the kings.

Balthazar arose from the bench to thank the dancers.

"Thank you, good friends,
  for your dances and your gifts.
  But now we must bid you good night.
  We have little time for sleep and a long journey ahead."

The shepherds replied,

"Good night, my good kings, good night and farewell.
  The pale stones foretell that dawn is in sight.
  Good night, my good kings, good night and farewell.
  The night wind foretells that day will be bright."

The shepherds passed before the three kings, bowing as they departed. Amahl's mother said good night to them at the door

and stood there for a moment, watching them go down the road. The lanterns twinkled among the hills and Amahl could hear their voices still calling, "Good night."

When Amahl's mother had closed the door, she said good night to the kings and prepared for herself a pallet of sheepskins on the floor. While she was busy, Amahl seized the opportunity to speak softly to Kaspar. He said, forgetting that the old king was deaf,

"Excuse me, sir: Amongst your magic stones is there—
is there one that could cure a cripple boy?"

Kaspar tried to straighten his crown as he looked down at him. "Eh?" he asked.

Defeated by Kaspar's deafness, Amahl went sadly to his pallet of straw. "Never mind," he told Kaspar and tried to smile at the funny worried king. "Good night." He lay down on his straw pallet, placing his crutch at his side. His thin cat crept out of the far corner where she had been hiding and snuggled into the crook of his arm again. Above his head his caged sparrow settled once more for sleep. "Oh, what's the use?" thought Amahl. His mother had tried all kinds of charms—the snakeskin, potions of herbs, wearing a curiously shaped stone tied around his neck—and nothing

had worked. Amahl knew he was going to be a cripple for the rest of his life. He could hear the shepherds calling among the hills.

"Good night, good night,
   The dawn is in sight.
   Good night, farewell, good night."

Amahl yawned. He watched the three kings, still sitting on the rude bench, settle themselves for sleep, leaning against each other. Their servant curled himself up at their feet, his arms laid protectively over the rich gifts. He had placed his lantern on the floor by the fireplace, so that there was only a dim glow in the room. Amahl yawned again. He was determined not to go to sleep, for he wanted to see how kings looked when they slept. They looked very friendly, leaning against each other, as they shifted, attempting to get comfortable. But soon his eyes closed in spite of him.

Amahl's mother could not sleep. She sat on her pallet of sheepskins, thinking, and saw the first pale rays of the dawn from the hills slowly enter the cottage. Her eyes kept returning to the treasure guarded by the page. She said to herself,

"All that gold! All that gold!

I wonder if rich people know what to do with their gold!

Do they know how a child could be fed?

Do rich people know? . . .

Do they know?

All that gold! All that gold!

Oh, what I could do for my child with that gold!

Why should it all go to a child they don't even know?

They are asleep. Do I dare?

If I take some they'll never miss it. . . ."

Slowly she drew herself across the floor, dragging her body with her hands. She told herself in a whisper,

"For my child—for my child—for my child. . . ."

But when she touched the gold, the page was instantly aroused. He sprang up and seized her arm, crying to his masters. Amahl's mother pulled frantically to free herself, dragging the page into the center of the room. But she still clutched the gold she had seized from Melchior's brimming coffer.

The page shouted at the top of his voice, "Thief! Thief!"

The kings awoke in confusion and stood up hastily. Melchior and Balthazar asked in startled voices, "What is it? What is it?" The page shook her arm and shouted to the kings,

"I've seen her steal some of the gold!
She's a thief! Don't let her go!
She's stolen the gold!"

Melchior, Kaspar, and Balthazar said, "Shame! Shame!"

"Give it back!" yelled the page. "Or I'll tear it out of you."

The noise awoke Amahl, who sat up completely bewildered. But when he saw his mother being yanked about in the hands of the page, he struggled up with his crutch and awkwardly hurled himself upon the man. Kings or no kings, no one was going to hurt his mother! He beat the page hysterically and pulled his hair, in an effort to force the man to release her.

The kings and the page cried, "Give the gold back! Give it back!"

Amahl yelled in a fury, hitting the page,

"Don't you dare!
Don't you dare, ugly man, hurt my mother!
I'll smash in your face!

I'll knock out your teeth!
Don't you dare!
Don't you dare, ugly man, hurt my mother!"

He rushed to King Kaspar and tugged at his robe.

"Oh, Mister King, don't let him hurt my mother!
My mother is good.
She cannot do anything wrong.
I'm the one who lies. I'm the one who steals."

He hobbled frantically back to attack the page again and shouted,

"Don't you dare!
Don't you dare, ugly man, hurt my mother!
I'll break your bones!
I'll bash in your head!"

At a sign from Kaspar, the page let go of Amahl's mother's arm. Kneeling on the floor, she lifted her arms toward Amahl. Choked by tears, Amahl staggered toward her, and letting his

crutch fall, collapsed, sobbing, into his mother's arms.

Melchior looked at the boy and his mother with compassion and said gently,

"Oh, woman, you may keep the gold.
The Child we seek doesn't need our gold.
On love, on love alone
He will build His kingdom.
His pierced hand will hold no scepter,
His haloed head will wear no crown.
His might will not be built on your toil.
Swifter than lightning
He will soon walk among us.
He will bring us new life and receive our death,
and the keys to His city belong to the poor."

Melchior turned to Balthazar and Kaspar and said to them, "Let us leave, my friends."

Freeing herself from Amahl's embrace, his mother threw herself on her knees before the kings. She spilled onto the rug the gold she had taken. Amahl got to his feet, leaning on his crutch, his face still wet with tears.

His mother said, sobbing, to the three kings,

"Oh, no, wait—take back your gold!
For such a King I've waited all my life,
And if I weren't so poor
I would send a gift of my own to such a Child."

Amahl limped forward eagerly and said, "Yes, let's send Him a gift."

But his mother asked, "What can we send? We are so poor."

Amahl suddenly had an idea. Perhaps this Child was as lonely as he had been and his heart went out to him. What if the Child were a cripple like himself? He looked at the kings and then back at his mother.

"Mother," he exclaimed, "let me send Him my crutch.
Who knows, He may need one,
And this I made myself."

His mother protested, "But that you can't, you can't! How could you get about without it?"

She hurried to stop him as he lifted the worn crutch.

Amahl took one step toward the kings, then realized that he had moved without the help of his crutch. Astounded, he whispered, "I walk, Mother! I walk, Mother!"

His leg that had felt like a dead branch on a tree suddenly felt warm and strong. He felt the blood rushing through it and it ached, but it was a glorious ache. Amahl took another step, then another, then tried a little dance turn and skip toward the three kings.

Kaspar, Melchior, Balthazar, and his mother exulted together in awe,

"He walks! He walks! He walks! He walks!"

Step by step, Amahl made his way toward the kings, holding his crutch before him in his outstretched hands. His mother stood back, almost fearful of the miracle she was beholding.

Kaspar, Melchior, and Balthazar marveled together,

"It is a sign from the Holy Child.
    We must give praise to the newborn King.
    We must praise Him.
    This is a sign from God!"

CHRISTMAS EVERYWHERE

by Phillips Brooks

Everywhere, everywhere, Christmas tonight!
Christmas in lands of the fir-tree and pine,
Christmas in lands of the palm-tree and vine,
Christmas where snow peaks stand solemn and white,
Christmas where cornfields stand sunny and bright,
Christmas where children are hopeful and gay,
Christmas where old men are patient and gray,
Christmas where peace, like a dove in his flight,
Broods o'er brave men in the thick of the fight;
Everywhere, everywhere, Christmas tonight!

For the Christ-child who comes is the master of all;
No palace too great, no cottage too small.

WE WISH YOU A MERRY CHRISTMAS

TRADITIONAL

OLD ENGLISH OR SCOTTISH AIR

Happily

1. We wish you a Mer-ry Christ-mas, We wish you a Mer-ry Christ-mas, We wish you a Mer-ry Christ-mas, And a Hap-py New Year!

Refrain

Good tid-ings we bring to you and your kin; Good tid-ings for Christ-mas And a Hap-py New Year!

2. Now bring us some figgy pudding,
   Now bring us some figgy pudding,
   Now bring us some figgy pudding,
   And bring it out here.
   Refrain

3. We won't go until we get some,
   We won't go until we get some,
   We won't go until we get some,
   So bring some out here.
   Refrain

4. We all love figgy pudding,
   We all love figgy pudding,
   We all love figgy pudding,
   So bring some out here.
   Refrain

5. We wish you a Merry Christmas,
   We wish you a Merry Christmas,
   We wish you a Merry Christmas,
   And a Happy New Year!
   Refrain

ACKNOWLEDGMENTS

Every effort has been made to trace the ownership of all copyrighted material and to secure necessary permissions to reprint these selections. In the event of any questions arising as to the use of any material, the editor and the publisher, while expressing regret for any inadvertent error, will be happy to make the necessary correction in future printings. Thanks are due to the following for permission to reprint the selections below:

Amahl and the Night Visitors words and music by Gian-Carlo Menotti. Copyright © 1951 by G. Schirmer, Inc. International Copyright secured. All rights reserved. Reprinted by permission.

"The Ballad of Befana" Copyright © 1958 by Phyllis McGinley. Reprinted by permission of Curtis Brown, Ltd.

The Best Christmas Pageant Ever Copyright © 1972 by Barbara Robinson. Used by permission of HarperCollins Publishers.

The Best Gift of All reprinted by permission from *Christmas Plays for Young Actors,* edited by A. S. Burack. Copyright © 1950 by Plays, Inc. This play is for reading purposes only; for permission to produce, write to the publisher, Plays, Inc., 120 Boylston St., Boston, MA 02116.

"Carol of the Brown King" from *Collected Poems* by Langston Hughes. Copyright © 1994 by the Estate of Langston Hughes. Reprinted by permission of Alfred A. Knopf, Inc. Reprinted in the UK by permission of Harold Ober Associates Incorporated.

"A Christmas Carol" by Gilbert K. Chesterton. Permission granted by A. P. Watt Ltd on behalf of The Royal Literary Fund. Reprinted from *The Oxford Book of Christmas Poems.*

Christmas in the Woods from *The Fairy Caravan* reproduced by kind permission of Frederick Warne & Co.

The Christmas Tree from "A Christmas Memory" by Truman Capote. Copyright © 1956 by Truman Capote. Reprinted by permission of Random House, Inc.

The Christmas Tree from "A Christmas Memory" from *Breakfast at Tiffany's* by Truman Capote (Penguin Books, 1961) copyright © Truman Capote, 1958. Reproduced by permission of Penguin Books Ltd.

"little tree" copyright 1925, 1953, © 1991 by the Trustees for the e. e. cummings Trust. Copyright © 1976 by George James Firmage, from *Complete Poems: 1904-1962* by e. e. cummings, Edited by George J. Firmage. Reprinted by permission of Liveright Publishing Corporation.

"Minstrel's Song" from *The Coming of the Kings* by Ted Hughes, reprinted by permission of the publisher, Faber and Faber Ltd.

"The Mother's Song" by Peter Freuchen, from *Distant Voices* from the *Book of Eskimos,* published by George Weidenfeld & Nicholson, Ltd.

"Shepherd's Song at Christmas" from *Collected Poems* by Langston Hughes. Copyright © 1994 by the Estate of Langston Hughes. Reprinted by permission of Alfred A. Knopf, Inc. Reprinted in the UK by permission of Harold Ober Associates Incorporated.

The Tailor of Gloucester reproduced by kind permission of Frederick Warne & Co.

INDEX

AUTHORS

INDEX

INDEX

POEMS BY FIRST LINES

INDEX

INDEX

ABOUT THE ARTIST

Appropriate for the illustrator of a Christmas treasury, **Gennady Spirin** was born on December 25, in the former Soviet Union. His exquisitely rendered watercolors are celebrated throughout the world. He was awarded the Golden Apple of the Bratislava International Biennale, as well as First Prize for Illustration at the Barcelona International Children's Book Fair. He has also received two gold medals from the Society of Illustrators. *The New York Times* selected Mr. Spirin's *The Sea King's Daughter, Gulliver's Adventures in Lilliput,* and *Kashtanka* as Best Illustrated Books of the Year. Mr. Spirin, his wife, and their three sons live in Princeton, New Jersey.

ABOUT THE EDITOR

Ann Keay Beneduce worked for many years as an editor of children's books. She now devotes her time to writing books for young readers and translating stories from French to English. She first discovered the extraordinarily beautiful illustrations of Gennady Spirin when she was attending the Moscow Book Fair in 1987. Since then, Ms. Beneduce and Mr. Spirin have worked together on several books. *Joy to the World* is their first collaboration for Atheneum.

Ms. Beneduce says, "The celebration of Christmas, both secular and religious, has always been important to me—both in my childhood and in my present family life—so it was a particular pleasure to work on *Joy to the World* with distinguished illustrator Gennady Spirin."